QUEST FOR POWER

QUEST FOR POWER

E. C. TUBB

WILDSIDE PRESS

CHAPTER ONE

They soared like the delicate spires of some ancient dream; slender pillars of glistening metal thrusting their sharp noses towards the distant stars. The dim light of a dying sun shone dully from the plastic ports and weapon-loaded gun turrets, throwing little shimmers of radiance from the long subtle curves of the sleek hulls.

They rested on the flame-scorched dirt of the landing field, rearing from the dirt and desolation, and seeming to strain towards the hidden glory of alien suns. Perfect machines, the end product of a thousand years of tireless research and embodying in their smooth perfection the hopes and dreams of a once mighty race.

The space fleet of Earth—grounded for lack of fuel!

They had waited for ten years. They had waited while men had driven themselves blind straining over pulsing machines and peering into the heart of exploding atoms. They had waited while the Empire of Man had crumbled and slowly disintegrated, broken by internal strife and the nearing threat of alien invaders. They waited until a new power source could be found, until once again their mighty engines could hum to the throb of power.

They were still waiting!

A man hung from the tiny, barred window of a cell. A big man, with the long smooth muscles of hidden strength, tall and with the narrow hips and broad shoulders of the born adventurer. He gripped the bars of the window until his knuckles shone white beneath the smooth tan of his skin, his entire weight supported by his shoulder and arm muscles, and stared across the desolate plain towards the distant fleet.

He pressed his face tight against the bars, staring with hungry eyes as the setting sun limned the distant ships with gold, painting the smooth metal with warm and luminescent light. He stared until the light had died away, until the gathering shadows dulled then hid the glittering points.

Wearily he dropped from the window, falling lightly to the harsh stone floor.

A short fat man sitting on the edge of one of two bunks looked at him and laughed.

"Again, Kleon? What are you looking for, rescue?"

"No." The tall man stared at his companion and strode impatiently about the narrow cell. "Why don't they come? Why don't they get it over with?" Cat-like he sprang upwards to the window, stared a moment, then jumped back again. "This waiting is driving me insane!"

"Easy," warned the short fat man. "That's just what they want to happen." He chuckled. "Why don't you be like me, I don't mind it here, especially when I remember what the penalties for misuse of power are."

"Misuse of power!" Kleon stared at the fat man and grunted his contempt. "You know better than that, Jarl. I tried an experiment, if it had worked, we would have been famous by now and those ships out there would be heading towards the stars and the work that has to be done. As it was…" He shrugged and sat down on the other bunk.

"We failed." Jarl relaxed on the hard cot and stared at the dimming shape of the window. "Five million ergs of power wasted, a ship wrecked, and we wait in jail to face the music."

"I wait in jail," reminded Kleon. "I was the captain, you were only the engineer; the responsibility is mine."

"No." Jarl raised himself on one elbow and stared at the shadowy figure of the young man. "You were on the right track, Kleon, I'm sure of it. Let me take full responsibility. They can't do much to me, I'm too old, but you can try again."

"Thank you." The tall young man smiled, his harsh features softening as he glanced at the fat engineer. "It would be useless, they know that I've tried to get official permission for the experiment, tried and failed. They'd never believe you, and I don't want them to." Impatiently he strode up and down the cell.

"Why are they so blind, Jarl? What do a few million ergs more or less matter now? Unless we can find a new power source the galaxy will sink into decadence and barbarism, and the work of a thousand years will be wasted. Can't they realise that?"

"Yes, Kleon, they do, but remember that the World Council is made up of old men, and old men are conservative. They are afraid of losing what little they have, and in a way, you can't blame them."

"Blame them! I—" He broke off as footsteps rang along the outer corridor.

Silently they waited as the heavy feet thudded to a halt outside the cell. Metal clanged and the door swung open. Guards, sombre in the black and scarlet uniform of Security, stood tensely waiting their hands resting on the butts of holstered weapons. An officer, the insignia of his rank gleaming dully on his shoulders, jerked his head at the two men.

"You. Outside!"

Silently the tall young man and the fat old one left the cell, the stern-faced guards ringing them as the officer closed the door. It thudded home, metal clanging from the self-locking latch, and tersely the officer snapped commands.

"Prisoners and guard, forward!"

He led the way, and the sound of their footsteps echoed hollowly along the dimly lit corridor.

It seemed a long way.

From ground level, through the cell block and past the guard quarters, where men lounged in careless attitudes on off-duty watch. Up a ramp and past the soaring windows now dark and limned only with the soft light from the distant stars. Still higher, level after level, along passageways once humming with busy life and now dead and deserted. Up ramps, then more ramps, and then even more. Upwards and upwards climbing steadily until their breath caught in their throats and the fat engineer wheezed with the exertion. Still they climbed.

They climbed through the great building for more than a thousand feet. They climbed until Kleon thought that they would never stop, until Jarl sobbed and fought for breath and whimpered at the pain of his sore muscles. They climbed until it seemed that they must have reached the very stars.

And then they stopped.

The officer of the guard gestured for them to halt and strode forward alone to a closed door. He knocked, and a grill opened, and a man's face peered at them.

"The prisoners from the lower cell."

"Good." The man vanished and the great doors swung open. "Enter."

Impatiently Kleon strode forward, marching past the pale-faced guard, past the lintel of the great doors, marching up to within a few feet of the polished surface of a wide table.

There he stopped and felt rather than saw the fat engineer being thrust to his side. The guards fell away, the doors swung shut with a hollow thud, and they were alone.

Alone that is but for the rulers of Earth.

They sat behind the table, three of them, all old, all thin, all withered and sere. They sat like shrivelled mummies, their skins drawn tight over bone and sinew, and their hot eyes gleaming like angry coals against the yellow parchment of their skin. Three of them. Three old men warming their hands at the dying embers of a once mighty civilisation.

Kleon stared at them his head thrown proudly back and his cold grey eyes filled with unspoken contempt. He stood waiting, the harsh lines of his young features limned by the flickering light of smoking torches, and as he stood the old men began to stir and mumble in envious anger.

"Kleon, once captain of half of our remaining space fleet, now criminal. What have you to say?"

"Say?" Kleon laughed curtly as he stared at the speaker. "What would you have me say, Landris? Would you have me beg your mercy? That I will never do."

The old man frowned, his thin mouth tightening into a gash across the lower part of his yellow features.

"Perhaps we could teach you civility," he said thinly. "Do you even now realise the enormity of your crime? Didn't the journey from the lower level show you just what your wanton waste of power means to our civilisation?" He gestured towards the smoking torches.

"Even we, the rulers of Earth, save precious energy. We use the light of burning wood to conduct the affairs of a world, our people climb where once they rose on powered elevator-platforms, is it possible that you do not know the true state of affairs?"

"I know that power is in short supply, but not that short." Kleon stared contemptuously at the guttering torches. "There is no need for this mummery, we still have electrical power, water still falls and the hydro-electric power stations are still working. There are still atom piles on Earth, and there will always be solar energy. I know that we need a new energy source, but we need it for those," he gestured towards the landing field, "not for domestic use."

"What little you know," sneered a man at the end of the table. "Tell me, do you seek to justify your crime?"

"Crime?" The tall man shrugged. "It was no crime, an experiment yes, but my intentions were good."

"What is that to us?" The third man, a wizened monkey-like man, slammed a weak fist down onto the table. "Five million ergs of power wasted, a ship wrecked, a ship that was half of the remaining strength of Earth!" He glared at the two men. "Death is too easy a penalty!"

"Death?" Kleon stared at them, then at the silent man at his side. "One moment before you decide. I must accept the sole responsibility for what happened, my engineer was innocent of wrong. Release him."

"No!" The monkey-like man glared at the fat engineer. "He should have stopped you, prevented your mad experiment, but instead of doing his duty he helped you. He is equally to blame."

Landris stirred impatiently on his soft chair. "Enough! This is a court of justice, the evidence must be weighed." He stared at the fat man. "Did you know what Kleon intended when he ordered you to connect the power to his machine?"

"Yes."

"Jarl!" Kleon turned and faced his friend. The fat engineer smiled and shook his head.

"It's no good, Kleon. I did know what you intended, and I think that you were right." He stared defiantly at the three old men.

"What do you want? Do you want Earth to die? To decay and pass from the knowledge of men? What are you trying to do with us?"

"Silence!" The wrinkled man at the end of the table half rose and almost shouted in his anger. "Be still!"

"Wait!" Kleon stared at the three men, and then smiled.

It was not a nice smile; it was the facial gesture of a man who no longer cared and it made the old men stir uncomfortably in their chairs.

"You know what I attempted to do, I had a theory, and I am still convinced that the theory would work. Why are we here? Because we used a little power, or is it because we dared to oppose your direct commands? You called my ship one half of the space fleet of Earth." He laughed, and there were tears of frustrated anger in his humourless mirth.

"Two ships! Two underpowered spaceships to defend an entire sector of space! What mockery is this? What could you hope for those ships to do?" He paused and rested his hands on the edge of the polished table. Steadily he looked at them, at their wasted features, their sere and wrinkled skin, at their hate filled eyes, and his young features seemed old as he stared his contempt.

"We need power, not the trifling amounts you worry about with your burning wood torches, your powerless elevators, your heatless cells. We need torrents of power, a river of energy, we need the power of exploding suns and disrupted atoms, where is that power to be found?"

"We are searching for it." Landris leaned back and for a moment his old features seemed to soften as he looked at the young man.

"Once I felt as you do, I was young and filled with the driving impetuosity of vibrant life. I was young, and I was optimistic. Power even then was short, but we didn't care. Something would turn up, something had always turned up, and so we drove our ships across the galaxy, visited alien stars and distant worlds." He fell silent staring into the dim vistas of the long-gone past.

"We wasted our power, we blazed a trail across the universe, and heeded not the warnings of our elders. We were fools!" Kleon stared at the old man, shocked by the vibrant self-hate in the old man's voice. He passed his tongue across lips suddenly dry, and listened to a voice from the distant past.

"Now? Now we have nothing. Our ships are grounded, our trade at a standstill, our factories idling and our agriculture starved for lack of artificial fertilisers. As you reminded me we still have some power, little dribbles of electricity, but we have none to spare. None!"

Jarl coughed, the sound strangely loud in the silence of the Council Chamber, then fell silent shifting restlessly on his feet.

"It takes little to light a room, to run an elevator, to warm a cell, but multiply that by fifty million and what have you? Ruin! Utter and complete ruin! We dare not permit the slightest waste of power and so we burn wood for light and warmth. We have no coal; we have no oil; we have no trans-uranic elements to restock the atomic piles. We have nothing, nothing except hope and even that is dying, and with it dies the race of Man!"

"Then now is the time for desperate measures!" Kleon stared at the World President his cold grey eyes glittering with emotion. "What have we to lose? I have wasted five million ergs of power, well what of it? If I wasted fifty million, five hundred million, still what of it? If I succeed, then the problem will be solved forever."

"If you succeed, but what if you fail?" Landris slowly shook his head. "We are not monsters, Kleon. We have made laws and we must enforce them, but not because we have forgotten what it is to be young and impatient. We must consider the majority. If care had been taken years ago, if the insane waste of power had been controlled, husbanded against this time, then we would not be sitting here in judgement now. No. We do not like what we must do, but we must do it. Power must not be used without authority."

"Let me try again!" Kleon leaned across the wide table forcing himself to forget his distaste of the old men, his grey eyes wide with pleading. "I know that I can find the answer, I *know* it! Give me a ship, and crew. Give me twenty million ergs of power and the apparatus I need. Give me these things, and I will give you eternal power. Power for the grounded ships, power for the factories, for trade, for homes and cities. Power to drive back the gathering clouds of a new dark age!"

Silence hung heavily on the still air. Silence and the tension of inner conflict as the natural heritage of Man struggled with the conservatism of age. Struggled—and lost. Regretfully Landris shook his head.

"That cannot be."

"Then…?"

Slowly the old man glanced at his companions, and slowly they nodded, a weary motion of heavy skulls, seeming to be like the ripple of weighted corn in a gentle breeze.

Landris sighed and licked thin lips with a furtive tongue. He did not look at the tall, arrogant figure before him.

"Kleon, one time space captain, and Jarl, one time engineer, the sentence of this court is that you suffer the extreme penalty for…"

Kleon smiled not listening to the solemn words. He knew what they meant. Death!

CHAPTER TWO

It was warm in the room, warm and brilliant with electrical fluorescence. Control panels lined the windowless walls, staring with their glassy eyes and betraying with the quivering of delicate needles the massed apparatus built solidly into the walls. A desk stood in the centre of the room, an instrument-littered surface of smooth plastic. A desk and a single chair.

Landris sighed as he closed and locked the door behind him. He stood for a moment staring about him, and a little smile trembled at the corners of his thin mouth. This was his domain. From here he kept in slender contact with the remnants of a once mighty empire. From here he listened to the whispered reports from a thousand spies, the muttered information which had made him the real ruler of Earth. The others of the World Council were puppets, mere figureheads dancing to his hidden directions, but he really ruled!

He slid into the single chair and closed a circuit. From a hidden speaker a soft voice began to drone, whispering thinly in the heavy silence of the shielded chamber.

"Reports from agents on Vega state that rioting has taken place on three industrial planets. Fuel shortage leading to shutdowns and resultant unemployment are given as the reasons. Rigel has reduced its fleet of starships to five, but still maintains internal planetary service. Rumours of a new discovery of uranium has forced the declaration of martial law within the system of Sirius. Antares has broken from the Federation and declared a total embargo on all exports. Barbarians have occupied the Fomalhaut sector of space, and all communications have ceased from that sector. Reports from Arcturus have…"

Wearily Landris opened the circuit and the droning voice died into silence. It was always the same, he thought tiredly. Always the same tale of steady disintegration and the rising tide of barbarism. This was an age for strong men, resolute men, men who could snatch at an advantage and by sheer force of arms or of personality, win a planetary empire. The barbarians did not stream in from outside the Federated Galaxy, they stemmed from within, and because of that they were the greater danger.

It shouldn't have mattered. The Federation should have been strong enough to resist such internal convulsions, but the Federation was weak, and the crippled star fleets could not enforce order and respect for intergalactic law. Once the vast concourse of Federated Worlds was broken, they could never be rejoined into the close-knit association of interdependent planets and systems again. The work of a thousand years would be undone, and the universe splintered into a broiling mass of jealous principalities and uneconomic empires.

Somehow that had to be prevented.

A warning light flashed red on the desk before him, and a muted buzzer droned startlingly loud in the heavy silence. Landris glanced at the watch strapped to one thin wrist, and pursed his lips, frowning with self-irritation at his forgetfulness. Deftly he threw a series of toggles, and slowly spun a rheostat.

Forces writhed in a wavering mist of blurred outlines before the wide desk. A thin high-pitched shrilling echoed from quivering metal as the surging pulses of sub-etheric current vibrated their molecular structure, building into a harmonic by resonance. Quickly the old man adjusted his controls and the thin shrilling died. The writhing ceased, the shifting turmoil of un-phased currents stilled, the hidden machinery droned deep beneath the chamber as they poured power into strange devices.

A man sat and smiled at Landris from across the desk.

He was a thin featured man with the high forehead and sparse hair common to research workers of that age. He wore a stained smock of dark green. Behind him loomed the images of vast machines, and he sat directly in a cone of white brilliance.

"Hello, Landris," he said casually, "did you forget?"

"Yes," admitted the World President. "I was thinking." He stared at the life-like figure of the man before him, dimmed a little by his own cone of brilliant light. "Anything to report?"

"The usual." The man smiled and for a moment Landris found it hard to remember that he stared at an image, the projected image of someone more than ten thousand miles away.

It was similar to television, but as far advanced from that early invention as it itself had been advanced from the crude crystal sets. Machines scanned with their electronic eyes an area within their focus and flung that closely scanned area on tight currents of sub-etheric force across half a world. It focused those currents, aided by delicate receivers and the image assembled as if it were in the same room. Landris stared at the green-smocked man, and he stared at the World President. Each seemed to see the other sitting before him in the privacy of their room, and each found it hard to retain the knowledge that they were but staring at a three-dimensional reproduction of the other.

"No progress?" The old man tried not to show his disappointment. "I had hoped that you would have discovered something by now, Stett."

"We are trying, but it isn't an easy problem. We need more power."

"What?" Landris half-rose from his chair, and in a distant laboratory his image seemed to waver and partly disappear. He sat down again, and once more his image was whole. "Impossible!"

"Impossible or not we must have more power," Stett said flatly. "We need at least an increased allocation of five million ergs."

"Do you know what you are asking?" The World President tried to control his anger. "Five million ergs! I have just sentenced two men to death for wasting that amount, you must do with what you have."

"Then you may as well discontinue the project." Stett shrugged and stared coldly at the old man. "We can't do miracles. To ignite dead matter we need a detonator, a blast of energy which will literally jerk the electrons and neutrons from their orbits. We can't do it with what we've got, we must have more."

"I can't give you more!" Landris stared pleadingly at the technician. "You know how things are, if the others knew that I was diverting power to you they'd call on the people and overthrow me. How can you expect them to tolerate lamps made of clay and burning animal fat, torches of burning wood, and open fires for heat and cooking, when all the time you are using enough power to supply half a world? Be reasonable man, how can I give you more?"

"Easily." Stett smiled. "Just let us have a shipment of accumulators, you can order the ship to unload on the pole directly from Mercury, and it can blast off at once for a second cargo."

"No. Those accumulators are all we have left to augment the hydro-electric, solar and tidal power. Anyway, what of fuel for the return journey? You know that half of the shipped power is needed to breed radioactives for fuel, without that power how can we get a second load?"

"I can supply the fuel." The technician smiled at Landris's expression. "No, I haven't been hoarding it, we have managed to 'breed' a supply in one of the converted atomic piles. It took too much power, that is why we must have more, but it will serve to refuel the power ship."

Landris hesitated, biting his thin lips as he struggled with his own conservatism. The project needed power, needed it so badly that he had diverted more than he could spare to the polar laboratories. To refuse them more would be to waste what he had given but if he gave them the extra shipment and they succeeded! He stared thoughtfully at the technician. "Do you really believe that we can succeed?"

"Yes." Stett leaned forward, then remembering the scanning machines, settled back into the area of focus.

"It has been an age-old dream of all men, the power of the atom! Not just the heat and radiation of atomic fission, but the obtaining of the latent energy within each and every particle of matter. Once we solve how to burst the atomic bonds our problems are solved! A city could be warmed and lighted from a few grains of sand. Starships could cross the galaxy on a lump of rock no bigger than your fist. The universe would be powered by the energy contained in the refuse of its cities!" He paused his thin features alive with emotion.

"It isn't easy, in effect we are trying to burn ash, but it can be done, I know it can, but we must have tremendous power for the initial ignition of inert matter. Once we have forced a few drops of water to disintegrate, then we can use the heat of the atomic disruption to continue the process." The technician sighed a little at the stupidity of his listener. "It is much like lighting a fire, first you need to obtain a flame to catch the wood alight, once you have done that you can light other fires with the heat of the first."

"I am not wholly ignorant of atomics," Landris said coldly "and your analogy isn't a good one. Anyone can light a fire, but you are trying to ignite the ash or rather stone and rock. It isn't so easy as you make out, and the return may not be as good as you hope."

"What else can you suggest?" Stett smiled a little contemptuously as he stared at the old man. "Do you want us to burn wood torches—so that we can keep the sub-etheric communication channels open?" He nodded at the other's start of surprise. "Yes, I know all about your secret misuse of power, shall I remain silent?"

"What is your price?"

"I told you, a shipment of fully charged accumulators from Mercury. It isn't much to ask, after all you wasted more than twenty million ergs when the starship was wrecked."

"The men responsible are paying for that with their lives," snapped the old man. "In any case it wasn't twenty million, it was five."

"What?" Stett frowned. "I had the ship under observation and took careful measurements of power loss. Twenty million ergs, new scale of course, were lost in the explosion."

"I know all about the new scale," retorted the old man testily, "sometimes you must think that I'm senile. What's the good of talking of energy units in the billion billion? It is much more efficient to raise the scale, an erg is now what a kiloerg used to be." He frowned at the technician. "Your instruments must be at fault. I know that the starship carried no more than five million ergs of power, it is impossible that it could have detonated with an energy loss of twenty million."

"Naturally," agreed Stett. "Impossible, but it happened and so your figures must have been at fault."

"Perhaps." Landris stared at the smooth face of the green-smocked technician. "Very well, you will receive your power, one shipment only and you can threaten what you like but it is all I can give you."

"It will be enough." Stett smiled and glanced at something outside the range of the scanning machines. "If we can't solve the problem with the extra power, then I must admit defeat." He smiled again and gestured with one hand.

Abruptly he was gone.

Landris sat for a moment adjusting his senses. It always took a little time for him to shake off the too-real illusion created by the machines, and as he stared at the blank flooring before the wide desk, he felt a keen sense of loss. Angrily he shrugged and pondered on a new factor.

Stett must be wrong, but equally so he couldn't be mistaken. The man was too keen, too efficient to misread instruments, and far too intelligent to be misled. If he said that the exploding starship had recorded an energy loss of twenty million ergs, then the ship had showed that figure, but...

Landris *knew* that the ship had only contained a total power source of five million. Even allowing for a hundred percent margin of error, two hundred percent, and that was unthinkable, still the figures didn't agree.

He was old but his mind was still the keen instrument that it had always been. Something didn't tally, two facts didn't agree, and yet as far as could be known those facts were absolute certain items of double-checked data. One fact—the starship had carried only five million ergs of energy. Another fact—the ship had exploded with an energy loss of twenty million. A third fact—if either of the first two items of data were true, then the other must be false.

Unless?

Unless there was an unknown quantity.

He signed, the breath hissing slightly between his lips as he leaned back in his chair and stared blindly at the serried rows of instruments before him. Incredible as it seemed, yet it must be true. *Must be!* Somehow Kleon had discovered a method of increasing the energy potential of the starship.

The World President smiled his thin lips curving as he thought of the inevitable results of such a discovery. He could laugh at Stett, and the demands of the technician. He could stabilise his position and remould the galaxy into the Utopian dream of peace and security to which it had been heading. He could bring light and warmth and the close intimacy of easy and rapid communication and transport within the reach of all. He could weld the Federation of Man into an organisation which would last until the last star had guttered and died.

He could do all this—if Kleon had made his discovery.

Landris leaned forward in his chair, then halted, his finger hovering over a button. He hesitated and slowly relaxed into the padded softness of his seat. He remembered how the young man had stared at him in the Council Chamber, the expression of disgust and contempt, the natural impatience of youth with age. He had sentenced him to death, and now he wanted the full co-operation of the disgraced captain. He had poured insults onto a helpless man, and now what would the inevitable reaction be?

Thought furrowed the wrinkled skin of the old man's forehead. He had climbed from the gutters to become World President and one of the many things he had learned was never to rely on gratitude. Stett hated him, but the technician was working to discover the secret of atomic liberation, and one of the first things the man hoped to do with it was to overthrow him as World Ruler.

Kleon hated him, what would be his reaction to freedom and a humble request?

Yet he could not let the man die. Not with the unexplained mystery of the unaccounted fifteen million ergs of energy loss. Not while there was just the slenderest hope that impossible though it may seem, the disgraced captain held the key for which any race in the galaxy would have paid whatever he asked.

Such a man was dangerous!

Landris hesitated as he stared at the buttons before him, then smiled as his ready brain found the obvious solution. The man could not be set free, neither could he be executed, therefore he must be held, and held in a safe place. Gently he pressed a button before him.

"Yes, sir?"

"Connect me with the Captain of the Guard."

"Yes, sir." The intercom hummed a moment, then…

"Captain of the Guard here."

"Landris. Instructions as to disposal of prisoners Kleon and," he frowned in thought for a moment, "a fat man named Jarl."

"Yes?"

"They are not to be executed. Understand that. They are to be kept alive at all costs. Hold them until a power ship leaves for Mercury. That is all."

"Mercury?" Surprise sounded in the captain's voice, then he chuckled. "I understand, sir."

The intercom clicked into silence.

CHAPTER THREE

There were five of them on the ship, five prisoners cooped in a tiny cabin bare but for five hammocks, a water faucet, and a small annexe. Kleon stood wide-legged on the quivering metal floor plates and felt his body thrum in sympathy to the thundering rockets hurling them through space.

Jarl peered from over the edge of his hammock and grunted as he felt the acceleration pressure thrust against his fat.

"What next, Kleon? First, we've an appointment with a firing party, then a last minute reprieve and here we are in space. Where are we bound?"

"Don't you know?" A burly man swung his legs from his hammock and dropped lightly to the floor. He grinned at them, his ugly features topped with a mass of unruly red hair.

"No."

"You surprise me." The redhead jerked a thumb towards the other two. "They know, why don't you?"

"We don't." Kleon was deliberately curt. "Where are we going?"

"Mercury."

"Mercury?"

"Yes, haven't you even heard of the place? The nearest planet to the sun, the place where they send all the so-called criminals, the food thieves, the work-shy, the poor fools who try to read a book by electricity instead of an animal-fat lamp."

"I have heard of it," said Kleon quietly. He stared at the other two men. One was very old, a thin wizened little man with a mane of white hair and vague blue eyes. The other was a swarthy short man with a scarred cheek.

"I'm Branson, my friends call me Red." The big man introduced himself. "He's Darko, I don't know his other name, I doubt whether he ever had one. The old man is Professor Hermitage, naturally we call him Prof." He stared at the young captain. "What did they send you to the 'Hell Planet' for?"

"Having an accident." Kleon stretched himself and smiled at the big man. "What do we do on Mercury, Red?"

"Work!" The big man stared at the lithe figure of tall adventurer. "You should last well, slim men always do, fatty and the Prof. will fade pretty quick."

"What sort of work?"

"Humping accumulators mostly. We connect them to the thermocouples and disconnect them when charged. You know that the entire twilight zone is a giant powerhouse?"

"I've heard something about it."

"You'll do more than just hear about it," promised the big man grimly. "The administration domes aren't too bad, at least a man can live in them, but the prisoners quarters aren't like that at all. If the heat doesn't get you, the radiation will—that is if you can stand the strain of constant work long enough for it to affect you."

"You seem to know quite a bit about it," Kleon said quietly. He stared at the big man. "How did you learn what you have just told us?"

"I was a pilot on the power ship run, I actually navigated one of these ships; at least I did until I got into an argument with a man in a tavern."

"What happened?"

"He went to hospital, and I drew ten years on Mercury."

"I see," Kleon stared at the old man, "and him?"

"Misuse of power, he was caught reading a book by the light of a stolen accumulator. Darko is a mystery, but I think that he was caught smuggling food, unregistered food that is, from the agricultural areas." Branson stared curiously at the tall young man. "Why are you here?"

"I was captain of a starship; Jarl was my engineer. We had an accident and wasted some power." Kleon was deliberately vague. He shook himself, half angry with the quivering vessel and missing the shrilling whine of the great starships. The big man smiled at his expression.

"Slow, aren't they? These ships I mean. If they only had the power, they could operate the nulgrav drive and we'd be there in no time at all, but they haven't got the power."

"Is this a starship then?" Kleon looked his surprise. "I'd thought that they were all grounded."

"Most of them are, but they are the only ships with enough cargo space to make this run worthwhile. They have stripped the fittings of course. All the armament except one turret, the cabins, most of the intergalactic navigational instruments. They've just left the hull and the nulgrav drive engines, they are built into the hull anyway. The rest of the space is filled with discharged accumulators for recharging."

"I see," said Kleon quietly. "It's going to be a long journey then."

"Yes." Red glanced upwards as a warning siren echoed throughout the ship. "Better get back into the hammocks, they're going to cut the rocket drive and coast the rest of the way."

He swung himself into his webbing as he spoke and Kleon followed his example. He had had some experience of free fall and knew what to expect.

It wasn't long in coming.

The siren wailed again, a long whine then three short ones and as the mechanical voice died, so did the thunder of the rockets.

Silence fell, silence and the horrible nausea of free fall.

It was something impossible ever to get used to. Space hardened veterans suffered equally with the tyros, and both suffered literal hell. Weight vanished. The constant pull of gravitation and with it went the sense of balance, the sense of direction, and almost sanity itself. Without the steady downward pull of gravity, the delicate balancing mechanism in each ear was thrown out of adjustment. The result was a continuous sense of falling, falling without end. The eyes tried to correct the false impression, they sent messages to the brain that were at variance to other sense impressions and the result was internal conflict ending in nausea.

Nausea! A stomach-wrenching thing twisting and churning in constant heaves and retchings. Seasickness was as nothing to it—and seasickness was bad enough. It made eating an impossibility, sleeping a hopeless dream, even drinking required a terrible effort of will. It could lead to neurosis, to physical breakdown, it could even lead to death.

Kleon felt the first stirrings of his stomach and grabbed at the rubber bag, standard equipment on all spaceships. He threw up the remains of his last meal, then the watery juices remaining, then lay writhing with the dry heaves. His eyes blurred as he writhed on the wide webbing of the hammock every muscular motion sending him from the supporting webbing. If he hadn't been strapped down, he would have floated helplessly in the heavy air of the tiny cabin.

He groaned, the sweat streaming from every pore, and his head throbbed with savage pain. Dimly he could hear the reactions of the others, the grunting from Jarl and the big redheaded man. The stream of obscene curses from the short swarthy man, and a thin high whining from the old professor.

Time seemed to have stopped, to have slowed so that each second stretched to an hour and each hour to an eternity. Kleon knew that his time sense was warped by the sensation of free fall. Now it seemed to have slowed, later it would veer the other way, so that they would lie log-like and helplessly concerned with their own physical discomforts. Then they would be in a coma, a mindless semi-conscious state in which they would lie as if in a vacuum, their reactions slowed, their overstrained bodies and maladjusted minds resting in revolt from trying to understand the impossible.

Darkness would have helped, it would have prevented their eyes from relaying conflicting impressions to the mind, but with darkness the sensation of eternal fall grew too strong. Men had died from sheer fear because they had become convinced that they were falling into a bottomless abyss, the lights were the lesser of two evils.

Kleon forced himself to adjust his mind as he rested full length, feeling the alternate tug of the confining straps and the broad webbing of the hammock. A psychologist had once told him that the dangers of free fall were not physical but mental. If a mental adjustment could be made so that intelligent reasoning could replace the sense impressions, then the horrors of nausea would vanish. If a man could convince his body by cold logic that it was *not* falling, force himself to ignore the messages from his eyes and ears, then free fall would become a delightful sensation, instead of the dreaded thing it was.

For the hundredth time since he had listened to the psychologist Kleon tried to obtain that mental adjustment. He deliberately blanked his mind, ignored the impression of constant fall, and closed his eyes against the shifting lines of the cabin. Slowly he seemed to gain some measure of calm.

Jarl and the big man had fallen silent, both veterans of space they knew that all they could hope for was a short journey and accepted their physical discomfort with iron stoicism. The short swarthy man had ceased his cursing and his thin whine rang incessantly from the metal of floor plates and bulkheads. Kleon forced himself to ignore the irritating sound. The old man…?

Abruptly Kleon sat upright on his swaying hammock, his eyes wide and his ears straining to catch the faint sound. Silence save for the thin monotonous whine, then…

"Hermitage!" he called. "Professor, are you all right?"

Tensely he sat waiting, fighting the nausea tearing at his quivering stomach, clinging to the webbing and listening, listening.

It came again, a thin faint cry, a bubbling whisper of a ghost-scream muted and as weak as a dead hope. It came from the old man.

Swiftly Kleon unfastened the straps confining him to the hammock, and with a jerk of his legs drifted across the cabin. Jarl lifted his head as the tall young man passed his hammock.

"Kleon! What's the matter?"

"The old man, he's dying. Quick, help me if you can."

"Dying?" Branson twisted as he stared at the old professor. Kleon looked at him, his face grey as he clung grimly to the edge of the old man's hammock.

"Yes. Can you help?"

"I'll try." Retching and heaving the big man joined Kleon and the fat engineer. Together they stooped over the old man and shuddered at what they saw.

Hermitage was dying!

He rested, wide-eyed and immobile, suspended between the webbing and the confining straps. His mouth hung slack and lifeless, drooling as that of an idiot, and a thin trickle of blood broke into tiny droplets as it left his lips. Sweat glistened on his thin features, a thin mist of extruded moisture softening the ghastly grey-green pallor of his skin. His hair clung to his skull, dampened and stuck to his perspiring flesh, and the small sounds which trickled from between his colourless lips was horrible to hear.

Branson looked at the young adventurer.

"Unless we can get gravity he'll die." He swallowed as clung to the webbing. "I don't know how much longer he can last, and the journey isn't over yet."

"Can we contact the captain?"

"No. The intercom has been disconnected; we operate by siren." Red clenched his big hands. "What can we do?"

"Wait!" Kleon frowned in thought. "We must give him the semblance of gravity, a little would do, he only needs to read-just his synapses." He stared about the bare cabin. "If we could give him even a few minutes of normalcy, a brief respite from his nausea, ten minutes would do it."

Jarl retched and shuddered as he clutched at his stomach, his fat quivering as he moved. He jerked and gasped with fear as he drifted helplessly towards the centre of the room. Wildly he thrashed his arms as he tried to regain his grip on the hammock, but lack of traction kept him where he was. Kleon reached out and pulled the fat engineer towards the webbing and with a grunt of relief Jarl grabbed hold of the material.

"Hold onto me," he gasped. "Hold tight!"

"I've got you," snapped Kleon. He frowned as he stared around the cabin. "That gives me an idea! Listen! If we can spin the old man, spin him fast enough, the centrifugal force will provide a synthetic gravity pull." He stared at the others. "Can we do it? It may save his life!"

"Let's try," grunted Branson. Rapidly they tore a hammock from its fastenings, lashing one end around Kleon's arms and shoulders. The other they fastened to the old man. He moaned a little as they moved him, and the sound spurred them to greater speed.

Carefully Jarl and Branson anchored their legs, lashing them with the retaining straps from the hammocks, and fastening the lashings to ring bolts set in the bulkheads. Grimly they clutched hold of Kleon's legs, then waited, fighting the nausea twisting their insides.

"Ready?"

Kleon nodded, then with a surging ripple of muscles began to swing the attached body of the old man.

Round and round he swung him, his back arched against the terrible strain, his legs firmly gripped as he rotated the hammock. Hermitage moaned, stirring a little in his fastenings, then quietened as the speed of rotation increased. Blood trickled from Kleon's bitten lips as he exerted every scrap of strength his lithe body possessed.

At first it wasn't too bad, the utter lack of gravity helped, and aside from his mass the old man weighed nothing. As Kleon swung the hammock, swung it as a hammer-thrower swings a hammer, weight, or its equivalent in centrifugal force began to tear at his arm and shoulder muscles.

On Earth it would have been impossible, on the lighter planets, barely probable, here it could be done. Faster and faster swung the inert body of the old man. Faster and faster, he circled, his thin legs trailing as he swung in a tight arc around the centre of the bar room. Grimly the engineer and Branson retained their grip on Kleon's legs, without their aid he would have circled helplessly at the other end of the hammock holding him to Hermitage, but their grip anchored him, and the wild plan succeeded!

Centrifugal force gripped the old man. It provided an artificial gravity, forced the blood from his head and back into his stomach. He moaned, twisting helplessly as he tried to sit upright, then slumped back as the fastenings prevented any further motion. A faint whirr grew in the air, the rushing of air against the rapidly moving figure of the old man.

Kleon stood it as long as he could. He stood it until his arm and shoulder muscles burned and throbbed with fatigue, until his head seemed to swell and threaten to burst with internal strain and his breath came short and ragged from his straining lungs.

Blood rilled from his bitten lips, and his eyes stared bloodshot from the grey pallor of his tight-drawn features. He gasped, shaking his head to clear his blurring vision, and forcing his muscles to continue the impossible strain he put on them. Steadily the rotation began to slow.

The faint whir in the air died, the blurred figure of the old man began to reveal more detail as his speed dropped. His thin legs began to trail lower and lower, then with a grunt Kleon caught the limp body in his arms and struggled to control the slight mass of the old professor.

"Help me," he gasped. "Hammocks..."

Gently they placed the old man in his hammock, then helped the tall adventurer into his. Jarl grinned, his teeth gleaming as he struggled to refasten his own and muttering as he strapped himself to the webbing.

"They'll never believe me when I tell them," he mumbled. "They'll call me a liar."

"How is he?" Kleon sounded very listless as he called to the big redheaded man. He winced at the pain from his torn muscles. Branson turned from where he bent over the old man and nodded.

"He'll live. He's unconscious now, but he'll live." He stared at Kleon. "I must hand it to you, Kleon, I'd never have thought it possible."

"It shouldn't have been necessary, they should have rotated the ship, given us artificial gravity by centrifugal force." Kleon shuddered as he began to suffer reaction from his too-great effort. "What's the matter with the captain, anyway?"

"Power," said Branson grimly. "To rotate the ship fast enough to build up an artificial gravity in the hull would have taken too much power." He smiled at Kleon. "Remember, I used to work on one of these ships, you don't think that the crew like free fall, do you?"

"No." Kleon swallowed and felt the blackness of oblivion begin to rise about him. He struggled against it, then relaxed. If he became unconscious at least he would feel no pain, no sickness, none of the burning agony from his overstrained muscles.

He smiled as the blackness closed over him.

CHAPTER FOUR

The sun rested a titanic ball of flame low on the horizon, a tremendous writhing mass of eye-searing brilliance more than seven times as large as seen from Earth. It blasted the sunward side of Mercury with burning heat and searing radiation, turning the rock of the planet into a charred cinder streaked and marred by pools of molten metal.

It had done so for countless years, it would continue to do so until the end of time, or until men could once again force the tiny world to spin on its axis. Until that time, life was confined to a narrow strip along the twilight belt, an area less than a mile wide. Here, life was barely possible. Here the torrid heat of the too-near sun was tempered a little by the frigid winds from the night-side, winds of methane and fluorine. Winds which swept across the night side frigid with the cold of space.

They swept by convection to the dayside and immediately expanded, gaining speed from the induced heat and nearing the low escape velocity of the small planet. Mercury was a dead world, airless, baked on the day-side frozen on the night-side, but it was this which made it so important.

Kleon stood by the open port of the ship and stared through the transparent plastic of his helmet at the harsh terrain. Thermocouples stood in serried ranks, their dissimilar metals producing electric current by means of the temperature change between day and nightside. Other mechanisms stood nearer to the swollen menace of the sun. Wide mirrors of sodium metal gathering and focusing the terrible heat, focusing it onto mercury boilers, providing heat to vapourise the metal and force it to drive spinning turbines.

The machines stood all along the narrow twilight strip, thousands of them, and each with but one single purpose. Power!

Power to charge the accumulators, to drive the ships and feed the factories. Power to provide the essential basic need of civilisation. Power to light the galaxy, to drive back the gathering darkness of barbarism and decay. Power to save the heritage of Man!

Kleon sighed a little, then stepped forward his fellow prisoners with him. Down the loading ramp, now almost hidden beneath the spacesuited figures of men unloading the empty accumulators freshly brought from Earth. Down the smooth loading way, and into the domed administration building.

Air whined about them as they stood in the vestibule of the air lock, and gratefully they opened their face plates.

"What happens now?" Jarl stared about him at the glistening metal of the dome. "This place doesn't seem too bad."

"It isn't," said Branson grimly. "This dome was built for the Solar Observation Corps. They liked their comfort and built accordingly. The admin staff lives here; we have other quarters."

He stopped and stared as a man approached them.

He was a thin emaciated thing, more of a caricature of a man than a man itself. He was hairless, twisted, with little red eyes peering from a deathly white face marred with ugly scars. He tittered a little as he saw them and hopped grotesquely on withered limbs his too-large head bobbing in an awful travesty of mirth.

Kleon stared and tried to hide his disgust.

"What is it?"

"A prisoner." The big man swallowed and stared at the tittering thing before them. "The radiation sends them like that, he's probably got an inside job; he could never stand it outside." He stared at the pitiful thing before them. "What is it?"

"Follow me." The cripple turned and hopped down the passageway. Kleon shrugged, and together the five men followed the radiation-scarred man.

He led them through metal corridors, lined with closed doors and filled with a soft humming from hidden machinery. Jarl stared about him, his fat features creased with a puzzled expression.

"Where are the guards?" He shook his head. "I don't understand it, we are prisoners, where are the guards?"

"What need of guards?" Branson grinned at the fat man. "What could you do if you did escape? Where could you go? Outside the domes you wouldn't live without protection for a minute, and even with a space suit you'd have to recharge your air and power." He shook his head. "They don't need guards, haven't the men to spare anyway, the entire planet is a perfect prison."

"Then how do they get any work done?"

"You'll see," promised Red grimly. "It's quite a system."

Their guide halted outside a door and rapped with a claw-like hand. A man called out from within, and the panel swung open. Together they entered the room.

It glistened with instruments, serried ranks of dials and power meters and the soft hum seemed suddenly louder as if they had reached the centre of the hidden machinery. A man sat behind a wide desk, others working at various instrument panels, but aside from the seated man none took any notice of the new arrivals.

"We'll make this short," the man snapped. "You've been sent here from Earth, sent here to work. You'll be examined for physical defects, then assigned to a labour squad." He stared at them with cold eyes.

"I needn't tell you that Mercury is no picnic. You'll do as you're told and do it quick. We have no time for shirkers and if any of you has an idea of escape you had better think twice about it."

"Why?" Kleon stared at the man his lips tight across his harsh features. The man smiled.

"You saw the man who guided you here, well he tried to escape. I don't know what his plan was, perhaps he didn't have one, but he was reported missing. We found him and naturally he had to be punished." He sucked in his breath as memory returned, causing his eyes to glitter with an animal-like emotion.

"He was put to work on the sunside, made to repair some of the sodium mirrors. He lasted exactly two weeks, then he was as you see him now." He looked at the tall adventurer. "He was no older than you when we caught him, how old would you say he was now?"

"Does it matter?" Kleon made no attempt to hide his contempt. "I understand what you are trying to tell me."

"Good." The man glanced down at some papers littering the desk before him. "We are short-handed here; we are always short-handed. Work hard and conscientiously and you'll be promoted to the admin building. Slack, and you'll wish that you had never been born." He stared at the old professor. "You had better remain here, you wouldn't last long enough outside to make your burial worth its cost. The rest of you report to section seven, the overseer will tell you what to do."

The old man hesitated, glancing at the others. "I would rather work with them," he said. "I may be old, but I am still strong."

"As you wish." The man behind the wide desk shrugged as he marked the papers. "The man who led you here will show you where to go." He jerked his head in abrupt dismissal, and the closing of the door muffled the soft whine of hidden machinery.

They wasted no time.

Barely had they been allocated cramped quarters in the prisoners' section, then they were put to work. It was hard work, steady labour but not as bad as Kleon had thought. Branson explained as they manhandled the heavy accumulators.

"This is the inauguration period; they can keep close watch on us until we've settled down. Later they will send us outside."

"I see." Kleon grunted as he lifted a heavy accumulator and connected the charging cables. Idly he checked the power flow and stooped for a fresh battery. "Is there much to do outside?"

"Too much. The radiation pits the sodium mirrors, and they have to be replated. The thermocouples need plenty of maintenance, and the mercury boilers have to be watched." He snapped the heavy cables to an empty accumulator and watched the swinging needles of the power dial. "It is a hard life, one that will drain the strength from your body, so try and do things the easy way."

"What's that?"

"Work in with the rest, don't make enemies, and always check every piece of your equipment."

"You seem to know quite a bit about the way things are done here." Kleon looked suspiciously at the redheaded man. "Is this your second trip?"

"I told you that I worked as navigator on one of the power ships, naturally I was curious." Branson laughed as he lifted another battery. "I never thought that I would be working here."

"I see." Kleon remained silent as he bent to his work.

It was never ending.

The sole function of the Mercury installations was to provide power for the energy-starved cities and industries of Earth. The titanic heat of the sun was converted into electrical power, power that was stored in accumulators and transported to Earth.

The accumulators were marvels of modern science. Basically, they were similar to the chemical batteries of an earlier age, but unlike them they did not depend on the interaction of chemicals to provide the current. They were storage batteries in the truest sense of the word.

A gas of peculiar atomic structure was confined within strong metal container. The gas was inert, and had one peculiar property, it could absorb electrical energy. It did by a warping of its atomic structure, and a fully charged accumulator was a mass of hidden stress. Power was pumped into the gas and as the charge increased so did the sub-etheric warping of the atoms. It was an artificial state and the gas was constantly trying to revert back into its original form. It could only do it by releasing the energy it contained.

An accumulator of twenty pounds Earth weight could hold one-thousand-amp hours at one hundred volts. The flow current could be controlled by two simple controls, and either cut to a mere trickle or released in a flood of energy. In effect, an accumulator could be used as an electrical bomb, releasing its confined energy in a searing flood of power and heat.

The accumulators which Kleon lifted to the charging rack weighed over one hundred pounds Earth weight, and each was sufficient to power a small factory for several hours. It seemed incredible that with the constant flood of charged accumulators from Mercury power was still in short supply.

Hermitage bumped into him as he swung to pick up another battery for recharging, and the old man smiled.

"I haven't had a chance to thank you for what you did for me on the ship," he said. "Thank you for saving my life."

"Forget it." Kleon smiled at the old man. "Why did you offer to work with us? You could have had a safe job in the admin dome."

"I wanted to be with my friends," said Hermitage with quiet dignity. He glanced up as a siren wailed, signalling the end of shift. "That was soon over, I had thought that the work would be too much for me."

"Give yourself time." Kleon joined the trickle of men heading to the mess hall. "From what Red told me, we can expect the hard work all too soon." He glanced at the endless stacks of accumulators. "I can't see why power is so short. What with the Earth installations and these batteries, we have enough power to run industry for a generation. They managed in the old days, and they had to work with equipment wasting more than it actually used. How can we be so short of power?"

"Shortage is always a relative term," explained the old professor. "We have more power now than any other civilisation in history, but we use more, and we need still more if we are to survive. It started a long time ago, back in the days of steam. Then the new power source seemed limitless—until more people began to gear their lives to that of the machine. Oil burners replaced coal, atomic piles replaced the oil burners, and so it went on." He paused while they shuffled into a low-roofed dome and waited in turn for their food.

"You can find a good analogy in the history of aviation. At first the aeroplanes used a few gallons of spirit each flight, then as the engines grew more powerful and the machines faster, the fuel consumption increased. Jet power came, and fuel was used in fantastic amounts, fantastic that is when compared to the earlier amounts, but discounting the increased speed and loading, it was a disproportionate increase." He reached the serving hatch and grimaced at the slop a taciturn prisoner poured into his bowl.

"Space flight came, and each trip used more power than would have been used in a whole year in the steam age. The ships improved, the starships came and with them the sub etheric communication system. Civilisation became geared to the usage of tremendous quantities of power—and it cannot make do with less!"

"I don't understand that," protested Kleon. "A man doesn't eat more, need more heat or light than he ever did. Why should we be so dependent on power?"

"If in the twenty-first century the atomic power piles had ceased working and the civilisation of that period had tried to go back to steam and coal, it would have collapsed. Industry had been built to use vast amounts of limitless power, each home had radio and television, electronic cookers, refrigerators light and heat from electricity. How could they have rebuilt their homes to use non-existent oil and coal?" The old man shook his head and tasted the slop in his bowl. He pulled a wry face and thrust his food from him.

"Better eat it, old man." Branson leaned across the rough table and pushed back the bowl. "It's all you can expect, and a hungry man is a weak one."

Hermitage nodded and forced himself to swallow some of the unsavoury mess.

"We are in the same position. The starships need power, a river of power, unless they get it, then our contact with the outer worlds will be broken. Earth itself needs every scrap of power obtainable; we could do with less, but the changeover will take time, and it will be a difficult period."

Kleon gulped his food, trying not to taste the artificially vitaminised synthetic protein. He sat deep in thought until the warning siren sounded for bed.

He lay awake for a long time.

CHAPTER FIVE

The suit was thick with insulation, ribbed and banded with metal and rough fabric. The helmet was a swollen ball of highly polished metal, marred with the slender thread of a radio antenna and fitted with a double face plate. Despite the thick insulation, the softly humming refrigeration devices, and the humidity extractor, the heat was stifling.

Kleon gasped and adjusted the controls on the tiny instrument panel set just below his chin. He slid a lever with his jaw and cursed the obsolete equipment which prevented fine adjustment. A voice crackled in his helmet, echoing from the receiver just behind one ear.

"There's the mirror."

He squinted through the almost opaque shielding of his faceplate and stared at the great bowl of one of the sodium mirrors. It was just over the narrow twilight zone and the full heat of the giant sun blasted and burned the entire area with fierce heat and radiation. Branson gestured towards him, the shapeless figure of Jarl beside him.

"Where's the old man?" Kleon twisted his body as he stared about the rough heat-shattered rock.

"Behind the mirror."

"Good. Let's get to work."

Hastily they operated the wheels controlling the alignment of the great bowl, swinging it away from the glaring orb of the sun. Kleon stared at the pitted and dull surface, and tightened his lips as he mentally estimated the amount of work required.

"Look at that mess!" Branson glared at the ruined mirror. "They expect us to finish the job before we return, what do they think we are, supermen?"

"Let's get down to it," snapped Jarl. The fat engineer sounded worried as his voice echoed over the radio, and Kleon could understand why.

The holiday was over, the labour of attaching the empty accumulators to the recharging cables—hard as it had been—was nothing to the work they now had to do. Their flesh had rubbed raw from too long contact with the harsh fabric of the suits, their eyes burned from too much radiation, and with physical breakdown had come a nagging fear.

Fear of permanent crippling disability.

Hermitage was the worst affected. The old man was a wisp of his former self, emaciated and weak with the searing radiation which had thinned his blood. The fat engineer was almost as bad, the wasted flesh of his once firm body had an unhealthy yellow tinge and his eyes glaring and sore with constant irritation.

Mutely they set to work.

Carefully they sprayed a cleansing chemical over the entire surface of the wide mirror. The fluid smoked and fumed as it struck the metal, boiling almost instantly into a heavy vapour and leaving a thick black powder over the once-bright metal.

"Is the sodium ready?" The earphone hummed and crackled from static as Kleon waited impatiently for the answer. None came.

"Hermitage! Are you all right?"

"What's the matter?" Branson came crawling over the edge of the mirror, the thick hose of his spraying equipment snaking behind him. Kleon tilted his helmet as he stared at the burly figure of the ex-pilot.

"Red! The old man doesn't answer the radio."

"Jarl!" Kleon tried to keep his voice calm. "Look at the old man, is anything wrong?"

Tensely he listened to the wheezing from the engineer, then...

"Kleon, Branson, come quick!"

Hastily they climbed from the edge of the great mirror clambering down the handholds and dropping to the cracked rock below. Jarl stood by the humped bulk of the sodium plant staring across the blistering desert towards the sun.

"What's the matter?" Kleon grabbed at the bulging fabric of the suited man. "Where is Hermitage?"

"Out there." The engineer slowly turned and faced his companions. "I don't know what's the matter with him. I was getting the sodium boiler ready for respraying the mirror, and when I looked for him, he was gone." He pointed towards the shimmering hell of heat and radiation. "I saw him vanish over the edge of that crater."

"Didn't you follow him?" Branson sounded peculiar as he shouted over the radio. "You mean to say that you let an old man walk to his death?"

"Wait!" Kleon gripped the arm of the big man's suit. "Remember that Jarl is almost as weak as the old man, how long do you think he'd last out there?" He spoke more gently.

"Jarl, how long ago did you see him?"

"A minute or two, I can't be sure. I heard you calling to him and looked up. A moment later and he had vanished."

"Good." Kleon stripped off the snaking hose and some other equipment. "I'm going to follow him, you get beneath the mirror, sit in the shade and stay out of the radiation."

"You can't do that, Kleon!" Branson swung and caught hold of the young man. "If anyone's going then it will be me."

"No. You stay here." Kleon shrugged his arm loose and before the big man could protest had headed towards the shimmering ball of the too-near sun.

It was as if he strode into the gaping maw of an electronic oven. Despite the thickness of his insulation and the overworked refrigeration units within the suit, he gasped with the sudden agony of burning flesh. Desperately he half-ran towards the edge of the crater, his feet sending little plumes of dust rising behind him as he ran.

Before him the sun seemed to expand until it covered the heavens with a sheet of lambent flame. Radiation stabbed at him, penetrating the metal and fabric of the suit as if they were paper, and he could feel his skin cringe as his nerves tingled to the savage energies.

Still, he struggled on.

The crater was a shallow one, a relic of some long distant meteor, now worn and crumbling from the constant heat of the sun. Something lay at the bottom, something shapeless and dark against the rust-coloured stone. Light glittered from the polished metal of the headpiece and shone in stabbing reflections from the face-plate. Hermitage!

It wasn't hard to clamber down the crumbling wall of rock, the light gravity aided him, negating the weight of his suit and equipment, and within seconds he was stooping over the crumpled figure of the old man.

"Hermitage!" Desperately Kleon shook the limp figure, "Hermitage, get up, man! Get up!"

A groan came faintly over the inter-suit radio.

"Hermitage!"

Impatiently Kleon stooped and with an explosion of sudden energy lifted the limp form of the old man and draped it over his shoulders. He gasped with the effort, the sweat running down his face and neck, stinging his seared and burnt skin. Grimly he began the return journey.

The rock crumbled beneath the thick soles of his boots, sifting like thin sand as he struggled to rise from the crater. The dead weight on his shoulders prevented easy movement and brought the blood thundering through his brain as he struggled to both retain his balance and climb the crater.

Twice he fell, the second time sliding almost to the bottom of the shallow bowl-shaped depression. Grimly he forced himself to his feet and tried to ignore the burning of his skin. Unless he regained the shelter of the mirror soon, he knew that he would die from heat and radiation burns, a wasted corpse on the sunward side of Mercury. He deliberately refused to think about the crippled thing which had met them when they had first arrived on the planet.

He didn't know whether or not the old man was dead. He didn't care. Every nerve and muscle strained to force his leaden body upwards, upwards to the edge of the crater and safety beneath the shelter of the great mirror.

He was almost blind when he reached it. Thankfully he struggled over the edge and collapsed on the harsh rust-coloured rock beyond. Hands gripped him. Gloved hands from space-suited men, relieving him of the dead weight across his shoulders and pulling him to the safety of the mirror.

"Is he alive?" Kleon licked dry lips and stared at the limp figure of the old man.

"I can't tell." Branson straightened and stared down at the young man. "We'll have to get you both back to the admin dome, after that dose of radiation you'll need treatment." He stared a little helplessly about him. "Can you walk? It would be quicker than sending for help."

"I can walk." Grimly Kleon staggered to his feet. "Let's get going." Silently they walked between the serried ranks of mirrors and thermocouples, Jarl and the big man carrying the unconscious figure of the old man. Kleon staggering and swaying as he forced his pain-wracked body to obey his mental commands.

He was out on his feet when they reached the glistening sweep of the huge dome.

Dimly he became aware of the thrust of needles stabbing at his wincing flesh. The sharp sting of salves and the cool sensation of a hormone spray. Instruments clattered against glass, and the soft voices of murmuring men echoed faintly against his ears.

"Will he recover?"

"Yes. We've given him anti-radiation shots and saved his eyes and skin. The hormone spray has taken and will heal his burns quickly and without scars. He will be fit for duty within a day; the plastic dressing is flexible and will peel off when healing is completed."

"What about the other one, the old man?"

"Bad. Physically we can save him; I've put him beneath intravenous feeding and artificial oxygenation, the usual treatment for such cases. It's his mind I'm worried about. Why did he walk into the sunward side?"

"Who knows?" The voice sounded very casual. "Perhaps he couldn't take it anymore. Better give him an inside job when he recovers. Any other casualties?"

"The usual crop. Suicide in section eight. Three men fought and two are dead in section three. Five malingerers, one broken leg and three cases of blindness. Nothing special."

"What's happening to the malingerers?"

"Work on the sunward side. They won't last long."

Laughter drifted around him as he felt the first thrust of violent pain. Kleon groaned, then tightened his lips against the pain.

He had to escape!

He hadn't thought seriously about it before, the change from expected death to life imprisonment had been too sudden, the reaction had made anything seem preferable to the total extinction of death by a firing squad. He had even ceased to think about his discoveries.

He smiled bitterly as he remembered his once high hopes, the wild hopes of a man who was certain that he could save the galaxy from inevitable decadence. He had been certain that he had the answer to the power shortage, so certain that he had tried an illegal experiment, tried and failed.

Must he always fail?

He had asked for twenty million ergs, a ship and crew, some equipment and a little time. So little, and he had promised a miracle. He smiled again as he remembered the thin old figure of the World President. Had Landris been right?

Was the steady progress of maturity better and safer than the brilliance of youth? Did he have any right to be contemptuous of age when he had done so little? He had promised much, and he had seen what his promise had led to. An entire planet devoted to the obtaining of precious power, and he was seeing just how costly that power was to obtain. Dare he use it knowing that it was paid for with the blood and pain of men?

He shuddered as a fresh wave of pain gripped him, and he moved restlessly on the narrow cot. His eyes were bandaged but from the muted sounds around him he guessed that they had carried him back to the communal prison quarters. His wounds had been treated, he would heal as well in his own cot as in the restricted quarters of the Admin dome.

A voice, low and careful whispered close to his ear, as if the speaker were terribly afraid of being overheard.

"Kleon, are you conscious?"

"Yes."

"Good, keep your voice low, others may hear us." Jarl breathed through his open mouth; the big engineer seemed to be in the grip of some strong emotion.

"Listen, you know the other man who arrived with us, the one Branson called 'Darko'?"

"Yes."

"I've wondered how it was that he didn't work with us, it seemed peculiar that four of us were in the same group and not him."

"What of it?"

"I've seen him. Kleon, he's horrible!" Jarl swallowed as he breathed rapid words. "I saw him while I waited for a check-up in the admin building. They've punished him, Kleon. Remember that Branson told us that the system here was one of reward and punishment. If we behaved ourselves, he said we wouldn't get hurt. Darko didn't hear that."

"What happened to him?"

"He struck an overseer and tried to make a break for a ship ready to blast off back to Earth. They caught him." The big engineer fell silent swallowing noisily.

"Yes?"

"They must have made him work on the sunward side. He's blind, Kleon, his eyes are burnt from his head. I wouldn't have known him, but for the scar on his cheek."

"That isn't too bad, he can always have his eyes replaced by grafts."

"On Earth he can, but we're not on Earth. That wasn't the worst part of it though."

"No?"

"He's insane, stark raving mad, tittering like that man we met when we first arrived here. I can't stand it any longer, Kleon. I just can't stand it here any longer!"

"Jarl!" Kleon forced himself to remain motionless on the narrow cot. "Get a grip on yourself man! It isn't too bad; we can last out a long time yet."

"Can we?" The engineer's voice was dull and lifeless. "You can perhaps, but not me. I'm dying, Kleon. I can feel it inside me. I'm too old to be made to work under these conditions, I can't stand it, the heat the radiation; you've got to help me, Kleon!"

"Help you? How?"

"Escape."

"Don't be a fool!"

"I'm not a fool! It can be done, I'm sure of it, but the others always failed because they couldn't handle a ship. We can! You're a captain, I'm an engineer. We can take the ship and head for somewhere out of the solar system, somewhere where they can never find us, where we would be safe!"

"It sounds pretty," Kleon tried to remain calm as he felt the surge of blood through his veins. "It sounds too good, have you forgotten that it takes more than two men to operate a ship? That is if we ever get a ship, and even if we did, where is the power coming from?"

"The accumulators! Listen, Kleon." Excitement tinged the engineer's tones. "Every ship leaving here for Earth is loaded with power, canned power, accumulator power. You know that they are converted starships, and they still have the nulgrav drive! Remember that Kleon, they still have the drive! We can power it with the batteries and head for Rigel or Vega, anywhere as long as we are safe and out of this living hell!"

Men moved close to them, and the whispering voice fell silent. Kleon shuddered to a fresh wave of pain.

CHAPTER SIX

The droning whisper from the concealed speaker sounded louder than usual, or perhaps that was because the information it relayed was worse than expected. Landris leaned his aching head between his thin hands and stared moodily before him as the whispering voice echoed from the confines of the instrument-studded room.

"Fresh riots on Alpha Centauri. A provisional government has been elected on the promise to devote more power for domestic use. Starships from the Centaurian sector have been cut to one per month. Agents from Polaris have not reported for three weeks. An unexplained explosion on Cygni IV destroyed three ships and half a city. Rumour states that illegal experimentation was the cause. Power failure has resulted…"

Irritably the old man opened the circuit with a sweep of his hand and reached for a thin sheaf of papers lying on the wide desk before him. Rapidly he scanned the columns of figures, then drew careful lines on a graph resting beside him.

It was marked with three lines. One blue, one green and one red. The blue line told of power needed, the red of power available, the green of power essential if civilisation were to progress to its high destiny.

The blue and green lines were complimentary, the red line lagged far behind.

He glowered at the flattening curve of the red line. It would even out, perhaps even fall a little as maximum power production suffered from the final breakdown of the few atomic piles, then…?

Then civilisation would also fall. The starships would rot, their mighty engines starved and useless for lack of power, they would be broken down for scrap, and once broken could never be replaced. He bit his thin lips as he thought of it, thought of the proud vessels rusting in a shipbreaker's yard, the gleaming hulls ripped and torn to manufacture ploughs and girders, rails and bridges.

Once let that happen and Galactic Federation would be but an interesting bit of history, a remnant of a Golden Age, finally to die in racial legend and myth.

It mustn't happen!

He stabbed a button with a thin finger and waited impatiently for the radio operator to answer.

"Yes, sir?"

"Contact the polar laboratories. Sub-etheric communication."

"Yes, sir." The operator sounded vaguely surprised and a little shocked. Landris grinned savagely as he caught the unvoiced accusation.

Let them be shocked! Let them whisper about his wanton misuse of power! If Stett had succeeded power wouldn't matter, nothing would matter, and if he didn't? The old man shrugged. He was still World President.

"Contact made, sir."

"Good. Inform Technician Stett that I will receive him in exactly thirty seconds." He opened the circuit and spun the rheostats controlling the scanning machines hidden about him.

As he waited for the twisting of the sub-etheric currents to relay his image to the distant laboratories, and for similar machines to bring the technician apparently within his room, he pondered on what he intended to say.

Stett had had long enough, men enough, power enough. It was time that he showed some degree of success, or he could help to replace his lost power by working as a prisoner on Mercury. Landris grinned mirthlessly as he thought about it, then stiffened as the familiar cone of brilliance sprang into life opposite his desk.

Stett smiled at him as he leaned back in his chair. He still wore the same soiled green smock, still had the same indifferent half-contemptuous expression. He leaned forward a little as if to shake hands.

"Trouble, Landris?"

"Yes. How are your researches progressing?"

"Well enough." The technician smiled at Landris's expression. "What's the matter? Do you still hope for miracles?"

"I hope for results!" The old man tried to control his anger. "Are you playing with me, Stett? I have given you everything for which you asked, men, machines, power, and I want to know if I can expect any return."

"Can you do any better?" Stett sat upright in his chair. "I have worked on this problem all my life, can you equal me?"

"Listen, Stett! The time for fencing with words is over. I want to know what progress you have made, and I want to know now! Are you able to give me proof that you are working along the right lines? Have you anything to show for all the power you've been using? When can I expect final success?"

"When I choose to give it to you." The man smiled contemptuously as he stared at the World President. "I admit the truth of what you say, Landris, but remember this. I know how to obtain power. I know the secret. I, and none other."

"Then you do know, you have solved the problem!"

"Yes."

"Then why didn't you inform me?" Landris stared at the smiling features of the man before him, and suddenly he understood.

"You want to overthrow me," he said slowly. "You want to rule Earth."

"I am going to rule the universe!" Something flamed for a moment deep in the technician's eyes and he straightened on his chair. "I have the power, and with power a man can be anything he wishes! I can refuel the starships; I can bring back prosperity to the galaxy. I can do all this—at a price."

"Ultimate rule?"

"Yes."

"You are mad." Landris slowly shook his head. "You have the old disease, the same disease which plunged the world into war time and time again. You seek power, personal power, and you don't care how you get it." He laughed and the technician winced beneath the scorn in the old man's amusement.

"Fool! How long do you think to remain in power? How long before a man with more strength in his arm than you have in your body takes it from you. You are a scientist, a man used to the ordered routine of a laboratory, what chance would you have against the intrigues of men born to a world of strife?"

"I hold the secret of power."

"For how long? Can you keep others silent? Could you yourself remain silent beneath torture? No, Stett. No. Come to your senses man, give me proof of what you have done, and I will see to it that your name is revered throughout the universe. You will have fame, prestige, a high position in a reborn civilisation. Isn't that better than the petty bickering of ruined star systems struggling for your power?"

"Talk," sneered the technician. "The whining talk of an old and frightened man. "You know that you will be deposed, flung from your position, left to die in some freezing hovel, and you fear that end. I shall ride the galaxy on wings of flame, my fleet of starships fuelled and powered by my discovery. I shall rule as no man before me has ever ruled, and you want me to give up that for the empty praises of cowardly fools?"

"You have betrayed us," accused Landris. "You have made plans unknown to me."

"Yes. The starships of the Rigellian fleet will come for me soon. With their vessels and beneath the protection of their weapons I shall claim all Earth. Once I have made it mine, then the universe will tremble to the march of a new conqueror!"

"The Rigellian fleet?" Abruptly the old man laughed. "Haven't you heard? Rigel has fallen to barbarism, who is to send you starships? Who can man them? Who can power their empty guns and fuel their idle engines?"

"You lie!" Hate flamed in the glittering eyes of the distant technician, and his lips writhed as he spat the accusations. Landris shook his head.

"No, I do not lie. I may be old and feeble, but I have worked with men too long not to have taken a few elementary precautions. Your men were picked by me, Stett, by me! There will be no fleet from Rigel, not if I have to drain all Earth of power to fuel ships to blast them from space. No. Civilisation is too precious a thing for me ever to permit it to be corrupted by a madman like you. You can be the saviour of civilisation if you wish, but you will never be its destroyer!"

"No!" Sweat glistened on the technician's face and neck. His expression changed, and Landris smiled as he noticed the trembling of the man's hands.

"Forget it," he urged. "Take what I can offer, fame, prestige, the admiration of all decent men. Isn't that better than their curses and the secret blade of an assassin? You have made a discovery, release it and see men regain their high destiny."

"No!" Something feral and insane. He laughed and the old man shuddered to the sound of the maniacal amusement. "You want the secret don't you," he jeered, "well come and get it!"

He turned and ran from the brilliant cone limning the area of focus of the scanning machines. Landris leaned forward, one hand outstretched, then as he remembered the illusion, sank back into his chair.

Waiting!

Waiting for a madman to make up his mind, for the men he had chosen to remember that they belonged to Earth and not to a power-mad would-be conqueror, waiting for the death or the rebirth of civilisation.

He knew that the technician had found the answer. Had found the secret of liberating the inherent power of the atom, a secret which would give all men everywhere the key to final domination of their environment. With it the emptiness between the stars would once again be lighted by the passing of many ships, outposts of civilisation would be fed and grow strong with new colonists, new industries, new and stronger ties of transport and communication.

If Stett regained his sanity!

If he didn't? Landris shrugged and leaned forward in his chair. Abruptly, the cone of eye-searing brilliance wavered, and Stett grinned triumphantly at him.

Blood marked his pale face, blood and the grime of battle. One arm hung broken and useless, and his eyes glittered with a peculiar shine, flat and dull as of a man who has travelled too far along the road of self-delusion.

"Well?" Landris purposely kept his tones flat and lifeless. The technician smiled, his lips writhing from his teeth.

"Watch," he said.

That was all. Landris knew better than to argue, he had done all that he could, the rest was up to chance, or the strange destiny that sometimes guided men. Tensely he sat watching.

The cone of brilliance before him seemed to swirl, to become tinged with smoke and the rippling colours of flame. Stett sat on his chair, his eyes dull and little specks of froth appearing at the corners of his lips. He was dying, the battle had not been too easily won, and Landris could only guess what ravaged hell lay outside the focus of the scanning machines.

"Now!" Stett grinned, opened his lips as if to speak, and fell forward, blood gushing from his open mouth.

Abruptly he vanished in a blast of searing flame.

Landris screamed, his hands to his eyes, feeling the skin of his face blister and crack beneath the savage gout of fire. Tremblingly he forced himself to lower his hands. The cone of brilliance was gone, the slumped figure of Stett was gone, the image had vanished and aside from the singed floor before the desk it could have been but a dream.

It was no dream!

His eyes told him that, watering, streaming with pain. The skin of his face and hands was not the figment of imagination, the skin was seared and blistered, smarting with savage pain.

With desperate haste he thumbed buttons and waited impatiently for the radio operator to answer.

"Yes, sir?"

"Contact the polar laboratories, use any channel open but contact them!"

"Yes, sir." Silence and the soft humming of hidden power then...

"They do not answer, sir."

"Have you tried every channel?"

"Yes, sir."

"Then radio the nearest air base. Have them send a jet plane over the pole and report back."

More waiting. Sitting slumped in his chair Landris tried to forget the smarting agony of his burned features and forced himself not to think of what he feared. Time crawled by then.

"Report from jet plane, sir."

"What is it?"

"The polar laboratories have disappeared." Surprise echoed in the operator's voice. "The pilot flew several times over the area and states that the surface installations have vanished."

"Anything else?"

"He reports that a tremendous crater has appeared in the approximate position of the laboratories. Photographs have been taken and will be forwarded."

"I see." Landris licked his burning lips, surprised at the sound of his own voice. "Did the area display any sign of radio-activity?"

"No, sir."

"Very well."

"Is that all, sir?"

"Yes." The soft humming of the intercom died as he opened the circuit and numbly, he sat staring before him. It was all too clear what had happened.

Stett had gone mad, torn between his insane dreams of conquest and the hard reality of fact. He had tried to win full command of the laboratories but had been prevented by loyal men. Enraged, he had deliberately released the titanic power at his command. Landris had seen the actual disintegration of the great laboratories, and it was lucky that he was still alive.

He sat, ignoring the pain that stabbed at his seared features while the keen mind hidden in his ancient skull raced on a fren-zy of speculation. One thing Stett had not accounted for. The disintegration had been self-extinguishing, the crater was non-radioactive, and the danger of planetary conflagration had been averted.

It was small consolation.

The hope of a power-starved Earth had gone up in smoke and atomic flame. Observers would note the explosion and ru-mour would run rife over the galaxy. Earth the mother world would be accused of barbarism, of wanton power waste, of in-ternal unrest a thousand things, but none of them would matter.

For the last hope had gone. The laboratories could be re-built, the machines replaced, the power restored, but one thing could never be recovered. Stett! Insane though he had been, yet in his way the man had been a genius. He had lived with a dream, lived with it too long, and when he had made his dream into reality, his mind had snapped with the false allure of absolute power. He had released the locked energy of the atom, but hadn't been able to integrate his own emotions.

Now he was dead, and with him the last hope of a desperate civilisation. Unless…?

Landris smiled, despite his pain he smiled in sudden relief. He still had one last chance. Hastily he pressed button.

"Yes, sir?"

"Contact Mercury, tight beam and absolute privacy."

"Yes, sir. It will take a little time."

"Hurry it up, speed is important."

"Yes, sir, but we have already exceeded our power allocation for this shift."

"Never mind that, do as I say."

"Yes, sir, as you order." Resentment tinged the radio operator's voice, the resentment of a man forced to sleep in an icy room, eat food from communal ovens and peer at his books by the guttering flame of an animal-fat lamp. Landris drew back his teeth in a silent snarl. Let them be resentful Let them hate him! He knew what he was doing, and if he failed, then hate would be a small thing to the emotion which would overwhelm him. But he must not fail!

The connection was poor, the radiations from the too-near sun filled the ether with blurring static, but he could recognise the strained features of the prison commander.

"Yes, sir?"

"Landris here. Those prisoners I sent you, a man name. Kleon and another named Jarl. You have them?"

"No." The commander stared at the old man from the flickering screen.

"What!" Desperately he forced himself to remain calm "Are they dead?"

"No." Anger twisted the heavy features of the commander. "They escaped."

"Escaped! You fool!"

"But…"

"Never mind that now." Impatiently, he broke the connection and sat staring at the blank face of the screen. His last hope. Gone!

CHAPTER SEVEN

It has been too easy. Sitting in the padded softness of the pilot's chair, Kleon frowned as he watched the dwindling ball of the sun. Around him, the ship murmured to the soft hum of power, the muted thunder of the rockets quivering from the metal of the walls and hull plates. Acceleration pressed him deep into the cushions, weighing his limbs and chest with added pressure, but he ignored it, staring intently at the glowing surface of the visi-screen.

"What is it, Kleon?" Branson twisted in the navigator's chair and grinned at the tall young adventurer. "Can't you believe it yet?"

"Why don't they chase us?" Kleon gestured towards the vanishing bulk of Mercury. "I can't understand it; surely, they wouldn't let us steal a loaded vessel without some attempt to get it back?"

"How?" The big redheaded man grinned as he jerked a thumb at the visi-screen. "This was the only ship on the planet, and before they could align their guns we were out of range." He leaned back in the soft chair and laughed at Kleon's expression. "What more do you want? Here we have a ship and crew, a ship loaded with charged power accumulators, and still you're not satisfied. What's the sense of looking a gift horse in the mouth?"

"I don't know, but there must have been a reason, those old proverbs had a lot of sense." He forced himself to smile. "How is the old man and Jarl?"

"The engineer? He's down in the engine room playing with his toys. Hermitage is resting, he hadn't fully recovered from his roasting you know." Easily the big man rose to his feet. "I think I'll go and check the gun turret; it may be needed." He grinned at Kleon. "I don't intend ever going back to that hell planet, and a gun turret in working condition can be a powerful argument."

He strode from the control room, his feet clattering on the metal flooring. Kleon shrugged and adjusted the main drive firing levers. Imperceptibly the weight of acceleration pressure died, and he rested more easily against the cushioned chair.

It was time for him to think.

Time to relive what had gone before, to weigh and measure, to check and verify. The escape had been too easy, much too simple and far too obviously well planned. It didn't make sense!

They had been working outside the living quarters, the four of them in their bulging space armour, loading the charged accumulators into the waiting ship. Others had worked with them, worked until the ship was almost loaded, then for some reason they had been alone. Quickly they had entered the vessel, closed the ports, climbed to the control room—and blasted off.

It had been as simple as that!

He sighed and stared at the shrinking ball of the sun with his cold grey eyes misty with thought. Mercury and all it stood for was behind them, now he had to decide their future. Lithely he rose from the control chair and followed the big man down the stairs.

Jarl looked up from where he crouched over an atomic pile, his face marked and stained with grease and oil. He grinned as he saw the young captain.

"Hello, Kleon. Where to now?"

"I don't know." Kleon stared around the cramped engine room. "How are we off for power?"

"The ship is crammed with charged accumulators, we've enough power to run a planet." Branson stood upright from where he leaned against the silent bulk of the nulgrav engines. "Where do you want to go?"

"That kind of power isn't what we need," said Kleon quietly. "How are we off for fissionable elements? The rockets won't work with plain electricity."

Jarl frowned and wiped his face and neck. "Not too good," he admitted. "We've enough fuel for the main drive to take us beyond the system, and we can coast if necessary." He looked sick as he remembered the ghastly nausea of free fall. Kleon smiled.

"We won't have any more free-fall," he promised. "Have any of you any plans, any idea as to the best place to head for?"

"Anywhere but Earth." The big man shook his head. "I've no desire to be sent back to Mercury." He looked at the captain. "What do you suggest?"

"We can head for one of the outer worlds, but it will be risky, the Interplanetary Guard still have several ships in operation, and they will catch up with us. I'd say head for the stars, get out of the solar system altogether."

"I'm with you there." Branson rubbed thoughtfully at his stubble-covered chin. "How about Rigel?"

"Rigel? That's five hundred light years away, too far."

"Then what about Vega that's only twenty-six. I know a nice place we could hide out on in the Vegian system, an agricultural world the Guard hardly ever goes there."

"How about it?" Kleon stared at the engineer. "Have we enough fuel for such a long trip?"

"I doubt it. We can activate the nulgrav engines from our stored power, but it's the ionic drive I'm worried about. We need fissionable elements to provide the rocket exhaust, and this ship is carrying the minimum fuel requirements."

"That settles that." Kleon stared at the silent bulk of the nulgrav engines. "It boils down to this, we can activate the nulgrav drive and head for the stars, but we haven't enough fuel for a long voyage. We can either remain within the solar system and run the risk of capture, or we can make for a near star. Alpha

Centauri is just over four light years way, so it will have to be that one." He looked at the other two. "Any suggestions?"

"What do we do when we get there?" Jarl slowly wiped the oil from his hands. "I don't like the idea of deserting Earth. They need this ship and the accumulators; power is short enough as it is without us pirating what's left."

"Do you suggest that we give ourselves up?" Branson didn't even trouble to hide his contempt. "What's the matter with you man, do you long to sweat on Mercury for the rest of your life?"

"Keep out of this," snapped Jarl. "You do as you please, but remember that I'm the engineer on this ship, and if you don't like it, now's the time to say so."

"Steady," warned Kleon. He stared at the silent bulk of the engines. "Can you connect enough accumulators to the nulgrav drive to create the field, Jarl?"

"Yes, but it will take about half of what we have."

"Then do it." He turned to return to the control room, then stopped as Branson gripped his arm.

"Wait! If we use half of the stored power to create the nul-grav field, how are we going to get back?"

"What do you mean?"

"Isn't it clear?" The big man flushed at Kleon's calm expression. "Listen. We use half the power to activate the nulgrav drive, then we use almost all our fuel to get where we're going. Right. Now what happens when we want to return to Earth?"

"We aren't going to return," said the captain coldly. "Isn't that what you wanted?"

"No. Why not head for Pluto, we can sell the charged accumulators there and live rich for the rest of our lives. Why waste something more precious than gold?"

"Hurry with those batteries, Jarl." Kleon shook off the other's hand. "You had better get to your post, you're a navigator aren't you, then plot me a course for Alpha Centauri—and be quick about it."

The iron ring of command echoed through his tones, the voice of a man who had once commanded one half of the starships of Earth. Branson flushed, then silently climbed to his seat in the control room. Jarl grinned, then grunted as he began to connect the ranked accumulators to the power leads of the silent engines.

Back in the control room Kleon slipped into his chair and with delicate touches of his hands began to align the sharp nose of the vessel. Branson called out the co-ordinates in a surly voice, and soon a brilliant star shone clear and steady on the cross hair of the visi-screen.

Alpha Centauri, the target star!

Impatiently the tall young captain leaned back in his chair waiting for the engineer to finish his work. He listened to the soft thunder of the pulsing ionic rockets, the vivid blue-white flame of their exhaust streaming behind them in a miles-long tongue of incandescence. A stream of ions speeded to an incredible velocity and thrusting the great ship by the force of their reaction.

A light flashed on the panel before him, and eagerly he pressed a button.

"Control here."

"Engine to control. Nulgrav ready to be activated."

"Good. Stand by with extra power in case of emergencies. Ready?"

"Ready."

Deliberately Kleon pressed down on a short lever, and within the bowels of the great ship a demon began to scream. A low humming at first, then higher as current surged along the intake leads. It rose still higher, shrilling and whining as the sound reached the edge of audibility. Still higher, and pain stabbed at ears and skull as the shrilling sound reached supersonic frequency. It passed, and the ship trembled to unheard sound.

Strain began to grip them, tension rippling along jumpy nerves and tightening muscles and sinews. Branson gasped, his mouth half open and his eyes wide and glazed with fear. Kleon grinned, his lips drawn tight across his harsh features, and thrust the lever down to its full extent.

The ship lurched! The ringing note from within the ship faltered and dropped several octaves, and the stabbing pain of supersonic returned to tear at ears and brain. Branson cried out, half lunging from his chair, them slumped back into the cushioned softness, his hands gripping his skull. Desperately Kleon stabbed at the intercom button.

"Jarl! More power, feed the engine more power!"

"A second, Kleon. The leads..." Grunting and the sounds of a man at frenzied labour came over the intercom, then...

The sound vanished!

A murmur echoed throughout the vessel. A soft sibilant murmur more sensed than actually heard. A peculiar sound, as if atoms were straining at artificial bonds, straining and whispering with protest as they struggled, struggled, and failed.

Kleon smiled and let his hands fall from the controls before him. He listened to the soft rustling from the hull, from the walls and deck plates, from every atom of his own flesh and blood, and smiled at the almost forgotten sound. It was the sound known to twenty thousand inhabited worlds, the sound which had planted the foot of Man across the whole universe, the sound which had given mankind the heritage of the stars.

The sound of the nulgrav field.

Sitting in the cushioned softness of the control chair, Kleon could almost imagine what was happening all around him. Natural law had been defied; the Einstein space-time equations rendered obsolete. The song of the nulgrav engines had freed man from the tyranny of light.

For man could travel at faster-than-light speeds. He could do it by restricting the essential component of the space-time equation. As speed increased so did mass, and at the speed of light mass would be infinite. It would take infinite power to move infinite mass, and infinity was something beyond the comprehension of men. That was the space-time equation of the Einstein theory of relativity, and it had prevented inter stellar flight for more than three hundred years.

Had prevented it until the nulgrav field was born in the unknown brain of a neglected genius.

Kleon sighed as he thought of it. Like all great discoveries it was fundamentally simple, but the theory of its operation was fully understood by less than one man in ten million. Each and every atom of the ship and its contents was within the area of the nulgrav field. That field had one peculiar property—it directed all increase of mass back upon itself in the form of usable energy.

As the speed of the ship increased so did the mass, but the nulgrav field prevented the ship from gaining mass. It was a contradiction in terms, something against natural law, and the solution of the paradox was simple. The thwarted mass increase was reverted into energy, guided by the surging currents of the nulgrav field, and used to power the ionic drive.

The results were fantastic! As the speed increased so did the potential mass, but the energy of the thwarted mass was guided and used to increase the speed of the ship. It became a circle a perpetual feed-back of energy, and it had given mankind the stars!

Branson grunted as he felt the pulse of the nulgrav field and looked at Kleon with a worried expression.

"Better not go too fast," he warned. "Remember the old man."

Kleon nodded. "We're safe enough until several light years, the capillaries don't usually begin to go until more than two light years an hour, and we're not in that kind of a hurry."

He set the controls on automatic and swung from the chair. "I'm going to look at the engines, you had better see how Hermitage is getting on. If he's in any discomfort let me know and I'll cut speed." He stood listening to the soft whisper of the field. "Don't make me cut speed if you can avoid it," he warned. "The field is drinking power, and it wouldn't do to be stranded between the stars if it collapsed. Not with the amount of interstellar traffic there is nowadays it wouldn't." He left before Branson could reply.

Jarl sat nursing a burned arm and feebly trying to connect a fresh group of accumulators to a jury-rigged power board. He glanced up as Kleon entered the engine room and gestured towards a smoking heap of fused metal.

"I misjudged," he said simply. "The field drained those batteries so fast they exploded into vapour. I got burned connecting up a fresh series."

"Much damage?" Kleon crossed the room to the medical cabinet and returned with a hypodermic filled with a scintillating blue fluid. "Here! Let me inject this nerve block, it will take away the pain." Skilfully he slid the needle into the great vein in the engineer's arm, and as the shot took effect, Jarl breathed more easily.

"Not too bad. We've used more power than I reckoned, and the field is taking more than it should, it can't have been kept in perfect balance there's a leakage somewhere."

"How much power have we left, stored power I mean?"

"About a third of what we started with."

"I see." Kleon stared thoughtfully at the humming bulk of the engines. "Can you rig a recharging device so that when we collapse the field, we can save some of the power?"

"I can try." The engineer grunted as he moved his arm, then looked surprised as the nerve block prevented pain sensations from reaching his brain from the damaged nerve endings. "I've been wondering whether or not it would be possible to drain off some of the reverted energy from the nulgrav field to charge the accumulators." He looked hopefully at the tall captain. "Could it be done?"

"No. If it could you'd be in the position of a man lifting himself by his own bootstraps. You'd wind up with more power than you started, and that would wreck the law of the conservation of energy." He smiled at the fat engineer. "It's a tempting thought, Jarl, but I'll be satisfied if we can save a little of the power, we used to create the field. Can you do it?"

"I'll try." Jarl stared about him, then lowered his voice "What do you think of the redheaded man, Kleon?"

"Branson? Nothing, why?"

"I don't trust him." The engineer pursed his lips. "I've been thinking, we took this ship too easily, it just shouldn't have been possible. Four prisoners, no guns, nothing but our bare hands, and we didn't even have to knock out a guard. Where was the crew? The captain? Where were the guards, the other prisoners?" He shook his head. "I don't like it, Kleon, I don't like it at all."

"I've thought about that," admitted the tall adventurer, "but what does Branson stand to gain out of it? Even if he did fix the escape, why should he, and how did he manage it?" He smiled down at the worried expression on his friend's fat features. "No. Let's just call it sheer good luck and leave it at that. After all, we have the ship haven't we? What more do we want?"

"A peaceful life," grunted Jarl, "and a ripe old age."

"You'll have both." Kleon stared around the engine room and nodded as he saw the racks of unused accumulators. "Listen, Jarl. You remember what we were sentenced for, don't you?"

"Could I ever forget?" Something shone deep in the engineer's eyes. "You mean?"

"Yes. I've a ship, a crew, and more than twenty million ergs in energy. I made a promise once, now let's see whether or not I can keep it."

Jarl smiled in sudden satisfaction.

CHAPTER EIGHT

The trading post was far enough from a centre of civilisation to be safe, and near enough for it to be within easy transport range. Kleon stared at it, noting the wide solar power mirrors, the high wind rotors, and the small turbine humped close to a shallow waterfall. He smiled and gestured at the unmistakable evidence.

"Look! They use power and need it badly by the signs. We should be welcome here."

"What makes you so sure?" Branson stepped close to the observation port and glowered down at the roughly built trading post. "It looks pretty primitive to me."

"No. They have solar power mirrors, and we're far enough from Alpha Centauri for the sun to be so weak as to make that an inefficient method of producing power. They have wind rotors and look at that turbine! I doubt if they produce more power than they need to light and warm the house, certainly not enough to provide local needs."

"I'll take your word for it," grunted the big man. "What are you going to do now?"

"Leave the ship. I want you to cover me with the gun turret just in case they have any ideas about helping themselves to what we own. Don't let anyone enter without either Jarl or myself, and not then if there is more than one. Understand?"

"Yes." The big man hesitated as Kleon moved toward the exit ports. "Wait!"

"What is it?"

"Are you armed?" Then as Kleon shook his head, "You'd better be, some of these frontiersmen aren't too gentle." He held out a pair of squat-barrelled flare-guns. "Take these they can be a very powerful argument in a quarrel." He grinned and gestured with the weapons. "Take them, Kleon. I'd hate to see you get hurt."

"Thanks." Kleon grinned as he thrust one of the guns beneath his belt and handed the other to the fat engineer. "Don't steal the ship."

"How far would I get?" Red waved and laughed as the thick metal door closed between them. Kleon shrugged and strode towards the rough trading post.

A man met them just outside the door. He was a small shifty-eyed individual with a three-day beard and a habit of scratching the back of his neck. He spat a thin stream of brown juice in the soft black loam and jerked a thumb towards the delicate spire of the starship.

"You own that ship?"

"Yes, why?"

"Nothin'!" He stared at them letting his little eyes drift from the soles of their magnetic boots to the tops of their uncovered heads. "Got anythin' to trade?"

"Maybe." Kleon stared at the man, his grey eyes cold and as hard as the metal of his ship. "Do we go inside, or do we move on?"

The man thought for a moment, scratching at his neck. "Better come in," he grunted, and spat again as they entered.

Inside the trading post was surprisingly modern. Portable Geiger prospecting equipment hung on the walls, camping gear, several energy guns and a few old-fashioned high velocity rifles. Shelves bore loads of canned goods, and the squat bulk of a transceiver stood in one corner, the screen blank and lifeless.

Around a rough wooden table several men sat and played with a deck of plastic cards, they stared with interest at the new arrivals.

"Have a drink," invited the trader. He thrust forward a bottle and glasses. "What brings you to this part of the universe?"

"Business." Kleon ignored the friendly offer of a drink, leaving Jarl to tilt the bottle and drink happily of the raw spirit. He smiled at the trader.

"What is an accumulator worth to you? A fully charge power-er battery of a thousand-amp hours at a hundred volts."

In the sudden silence the gurgling of liquor as the fat engineer emptied the bottle sounded strangely loud. The trader scratched at the back of his neck.

"Not much," he said casually. "Why?"

"Nothing." Kleon rose to his feet from where he sat at the table. "Goodbye." He moved towards the door.

"Wait!" A man at the end of the table sprang to his feel ignoring the trader's expression of disgust. "Have you many like that?"

"I may have." Deliberately the tall adventurer sat down. "Interested?"

"Now wait a minute, Jeb." The trader moved casually between them. "I'm a trader around here, if any business is to be done, then I'm the man to do it." He stared at Kleon, "What are you asking for them?"

"I've plenty such as I described, and some larger ones too. Ten thousand-amp hours at a hundred volts, fully charged and in the new light-weight containers."

"Where did you get them?" A scarred man glowered at the young man. "Are you one of these power pirates?"

"Take it easy, Sam." The trader scowled at the scar-faced man. "What does it matter where they got them from?" He smirked at Jarl. "I'll bet that the containers are unmarked, and I'll bet that a friendly drink could settle the price. "How much?"

"Equipment." Kleon stared at the man. "Don't waste your time with my friend, I'm the man to do business with. Well, do you agree?"

"That depends." The trader picked at his teeth. "What sort of equipment?"

"I want a Le Farge generator, a hundred-weight of pure quartz, half a ton of assorted metal rod, iron five nines pure. I want three tri-axial silver pentodes and a portable welding kit." He shrugged. "I'll give you a list, can you get the stuff for me?"

"Perhaps, but how can I get it up here? Ground transport's slow and erratic, and I haven't a flyer."

"I have," said Jeb eagerly. "I'll provide the flyer if you'll provide the power and spare accumulators."

"I've credit in town," put in the scar-faced man. "You can use it, and I'll take its worth in power packs." He breathed deeply as he stared at Kleon. "The money's useless to me unless I can power my farming equipment. One good harvest and I can replace the cash twice over."

"Is it a deal?" Kleon rose to his feet as he stared at the trader. "We'll work out the details later, but if you'll come over to the ship, I'll give you accumulators enough to power the flyer. You can have the rest when you deliver the equipment." He smiled at the men. "I can assure you that it's in unmarked containers, at least, the markings are not of this system."

"Good enough." The trader spat and scratched his neck. "I'll radio my agent right away; you'll have the stuff tomorrow."

"Right." Kleon nudged Jarl and together they stepped outside the building. "Just in case you get any ideas," he said casually. "I'm monitoring the ether and I've a gun trained on this place which could blast it to dust in one shot. Try calling the Interplanetary Guard, and that's just what will happen."

He grinned at the expression of pained surprise on the trader's bristly features.

Hermitage met them as they entered the ship. The old man has rested for most of the voyage and was now fully recovered from his ordeal on Mercury. He kept a stubborn silence about his reasons for running out towards the certain death of the sunward side, and Kleon didn't question him.

"Why have we landed here?" Hermitage blinked his weak eyes at the tall young adventurer. "Won't they find us?"

"I doubt it, the men we are dealing with have no great respect for the law, not in minor details anyway."

"They think that we're power pirates," explained the fat engineer, "but they're not worried about it. They need power too badly to ask questions as to where it came from."

"I see, but what do we want from them? Food?"

"No, equipment." Kleon slipped an arm around the old man's shoulders and urged him from the locked port. "Get, Branson," he ordered Jarl. "We'll assemble in the control room and hold a council. The visi-screens will warn us if any other craft comes too near."

Silently he urged the old man up the stairs and into the instrument lined control room. He crossed to the blank plate of the vis-screen and adjusted the controls so that the scanning field gave maximum coverage around the immediate area, then set the automatic alarms to warn of the approach of any large body of matter. As he straightened from the controls, Branson entered the room.

He grinned at Hermitage, waved carelessly towards Kleon, and fell heavily into one of the padded control chairs. Jarl followed him and sat next to the old man. Kleon leaned against the edge of the computer built into the control panel and stared thoughtfully at them.

"We've a decision to make," he said abruptly, "and it would be better if we could make it a mutual one."

"What's on your mind?"

"Quite a bit, Branson." He stared coldly at the big redheaded man. "What we decide now will affect our future, and perhaps our very lives. I suggest that we all give it some careful thought."

"Agreed." The big man glanced at the others. "How about you?"

"I'm all for it," said Jarl. Hermitage nodded.

"Good. Now as I see it, we have a limited choice of action. One thing is certain, we can't just keep planet-hopping, the ship hasn't enough fuel, and the Interplanetary Guard are bound to catch us if we attract too much attention. Starships are too rare to pass unnoticed and they will hunt us down as suspected power pirates or just on general principles."

"That's pretty obvious," grunted the big man. "The way I see it is to sell the ship and retire to some back-country farm or small city."

"We could do that, always supposing that we could sell the ship and get away with the cash. That won't be too easy, and we'll have to dispose of the ship in this star system. Alpha Centauri is too near Earth for such a sale to pass without question, and the sub-etheric communications have probably already warned the Guard to keep watch for a stolen ship and four escaped convicts."

"That needn't bother us too much. Starships are too rare and valuable for anyone to pass up the chance of a bargain."

"Agreed, but there is one other point." Kleon stared at Hermitage, then at both Jarl and Branson. "I don't know how you people feel about things, but I for one don't want to be exiled from Earth. I was born there, and it is my home."

"So what?" Almost it seemed as if the big redheaded man would spit. "This is no time for sentiment, you know what they will do to us if ever we return. The firing squad, or labour for life on the hell planet." He shook his head. "You do as you wish, but I don't intend spending the rest of my life in chains."

"How about you, Jarl?"

"I'll stick with you, Kleon. Whatever you decide will be all right with me."

"Thank you." Kleon stared at the white-haired old man. "What about you, Hermitage?"

"What can I say?" The old man stared at his quivering hands. "I'm an old man, I haven't much longer to live, and so my opinion cannot count as much as yours. You are young, life is before you and life is always what you make it. If you go back you may die, as things are it seems certain that you will, but if you stay here what will you do? Work certainly, for you are not the idling sort, but will you be happy?"

"Happy?" Kleon shrugged. "What is happiness?"

"Who can tell?" The old man stared down the dim vista of the almost forgotten past and spoke as a man speaks who thinks he is alone.

"The love of a woman? The laughter of children? The burning thrill of new discoveries? Who can tell? Each must find his own, and the happiness of one man is not necessarily that of another. I used to know happiness, once when I was young and the world was full of new and wonderful things to discover. I remember how I thrilled to the accumulation of fresh knowledge and felt the supreme ecstasy of creation as I built instruments more delicate than any before known. Research, that was my happiness, but is it yours?"

He sighed and blinked a little shamefacedly as he looked at the tall figure of the young man.

"Could you be happy without the respect of men? Could you live with the knowledge of what you are, a criminal, a convict, a coward? Yes, a coward, for a brave man does not run from his responsibilities, and yet even that may not weigh with you, but there is one other thing. You are a captain of space, you have thrilled to the song of the nulgrav field, seen the burning glory of distant stars and trod the soil of alien worlds. Could you be happy—without that?"

He fell silent and something seemed to enter the stillness of the instrument-lined control room. It was something intangible, something sensed, felt, an impression of some deep rooted instinct, an emotion as old as man himself.

Nostalgia!

Kleon sighed and slowly nodded his head. Jarl grunted staring at his broad hands. Branson sat silent, his eyes hard and watchful.

"You are right, old man." Kleon shrugged and straightened from the instrument panel. "I could never be content to remain planet-bound, never to see the unshielded glory of the stars never to see the beauty of Earth again. I am going back."

"Are you mad?" Branson sprang to his feet, his eyes blazing and his lips thin with anger. "What of me? Am I to rot in poverty while you take the ship? No! I tell you no!"

"He has a right to state his opinion, Kleon," said Jarl quietly. "After all he has a share of the ship and fuel."

"Fuel!" The big man grinned and sank back into his padded chair. "All this talk is a waste of time; you have forgotten the one important thing—how are you going to get back home?"

"Why…" Jarl blinked and stared at Kleon. "He's right! I'd forgotten about the fuel."

"You can't get back," chuckled Branson. "If you surrender yourself to the Guard here, they would either execute you or put you to labour in the local equivalent of the hell planet. You haven't enough fuel to return to Earth with the ship, so the choice is really a simple one. Either we live here a free man, or as a convict. Not much of a choice, is it?

"No," said Kleon quietly. "Not a choice at all, and though it may surprise you, Branson, I am not a total fool. I had not forgotten the fuel, nor have I any great desire to spend the rest of my life in chains. I have another solution to our problem, one which I think will appeal to you all.

"Another solution?"

"Yes."

"There is none." Branson snorted as he stared at the silent control panel. "I am a navigator, used to taking all known equations into account, and I have missed nothing. The choice is simple, remain free or give ourselves up to the Interplanetary Guard. Decide how you like but I've made up my mind."

"What is that?"

"I'm taking what is mine and getting out of here. That trader you bargained with will advance me enough cash to buy passage on an interplanetary vessel. I'll head for some undeveloped world and live the life of a rich farmer. You can have your glory, your high ideals, I'll stick to a full belly and a safe neck."

"As you wish." Kleon shrugged carelessly. "If that's what you want I can't stop you, but there is a better way."

"What is that?"

"To return bearing gifts." He looked at their startled expressions and smiled as he caught Jarl's eye.

"Earth. The whole galaxy is suffering from a shortage of power. Planetary systems are hovering on the brink of war, ready to kill and slay over the possession of some remaining beds of radioactive ore. Civilisation has reached the crossroads, one path leads to barbarism and decay, along that path lies the ruin of war and the wanton waste of energy used for destruction rather than construction. The other path…?"

"Is there another?" Hermitage spoke quietly as he stared at the tall adventurer. "I am a scientist, once I was the most brilliant man at spatial tensors, and I have worked for thirty years to discover a new source of power. I failed. Is there another path?"

"I believe that there is. A road leading to Utopia, a Utopia powered and guarded by unlimited power. Men can cross the universe, see new worlds, expand, even perhaps solve the ultimate secret of all. I believe that I can put the foot of Man on that path, but I need your help."

"You mean that you know of a new power source?" The big man sprang to his feet, his eyes blazing with emotion. "If you have that secret then the universe is ours. We can ask whatever we want, and the price will be as nothing compared to what we have to offer. Rigel will pay, Vega, Arcturus, a thousand planetary systems will beg for the secret, and they will shower us with wealth beyond the dreams of avarice."

He sat down again, wiping the sweat from his face and neck.

"We could rule the universe!"

"Perhaps, but that is not what I intend." Kleon stared at the blank face of the visi-screen. "It is a gamble, a tremendous gamble. I have pledged every erg of power we can spare for essential equipment. Either we discover the new power source, or we must admit defeat and pay our penalty. If we succeed, then Earth will welcome us with open arms, and civilisation will bless our name."

"If we succeed?" Branson stared at the calm face of the young captain. "You mean that there is doubt?"

"Yes."

"Then…?"

"I have hope. Once I tried an experiment, an experiment which almost succeeded. What I did once I can do again, and this time we need not fail, we must not fail! More than our lives depend on it!"

He stared at them, at the fat engineer, the big redheaded man, and finally at the old shrunken, figure of Hermitage. "Are you with me?"

Silently they nodded, their eyes alive with hope.

CHAPTER NINE

The equipment came next day, loads of quartz, soft iron, coils of wire and delicate fabrications of glass and metal packed in strong boxes. The trader supervised the unloading, his little shrewd eyes darting about the interior of the starship and scratching his neck as he chewed on his aromatic weed.

"Reckon that's the lot," he said as sweating men carried the last of the ordered equipment from the sturdy little flyer. "You going now?"

"No." Kleon gestured towards a row of accumulators and eagerly the perspiring men began to carry them from the ship. "I want to work here for a while." He stared at the trader. "Is anything wrong?"

"Not yet, but my agent in town seemed a mite too curious." He stared shrewdly at the tall young captain. "He might take it into his head to ask some questions, awkward questions. I'd rather that you weren't here if the Guard arrives to find the answers."

"Don't worry." Kleon stared after the flyer as it struggled into the air, heavily loaded with the precious accumulators. "If they come, we can blast off at a second's notice, and what they don't see they can't ask about." He glanced at the shrewd-eyed trader. "I take it that the accumulators won't be on show?"

"What accumulators?" The short man grinned and winked "Just so long as you know. I wouldn't want for you to get the wrong idea about me; that gun looks a little too efficient." He grinned again and stepped out of the starship. "If I don't see you again," he called, "a good journey—and come again."

The closing of the metal port cut off his satisfied smile. Kleon sighed and turned to examine the piles of jumbled equipment. Hermitage and Jarl were already sorting it out, the big redhead rested at his post in the control room watching the visiscreen, ready to send the ship blasting towards the stars at the first signs of danger. Hermitage pursed his lips as he examined the delicate construction of one of the pieces of equipment.

"What is your plan, Kleon? This Le Farge generator, is it to be incorporated within the field of influence or outside?"

"Outside." The tall young captain smiled at the old man, "You restrain your curiosity well, old man. I wonder if you would be as sceptical as the rest?"

"Try me."

"I will." Kleon tugged at a pile of soft iron rods, piling and sorting as to size. "You are aware of the theory of multiple universes of course, the idea that there is more than one universe occupying the same place at the same time. I believe that atomic physicists first formulated the theory to account for the otherwise inexplicable behaviour of the electron and mesons. They did not act as predicted, and the theory grew that some other force must be acting on them. The whole idea of course was then a purely mathematical concept."

"I know of the theory, and from my own work I know that it must be very near the truth. There is too much room within an atom, too many inexplicable variations in the orbits of the atomic particles. If we accept the fact that there are other particles, invisible to us, and following laws not of our own universe, then a great deal can be explained." The old man paused at his work for a moment.

"It depends of course on the vibration frequency of the actual particles. Just as some sounds cannot be heard by the human ear because of their supersonic frequency, and as the visible waveband of light is so relatively small because we cannot see the electro-magnetic range, so actual particles of matter could be at a pitch of vibration which would make them non-existent to our instruments. In such a case two or more atoms could be in the same place at the same time, separated forever from each other by a difference in their vibrational frequencies."

"Exactly." Kleon wiped the sweat from his face and neck as he leaned against the pile of soft iron rods.

"Now assuming that the theory of multiple universes is correct, and there cannot be much doubt about it now, what of entropy?"

"Entropy?" Hermitage frowned as he tried to follow the other's line of reasoning. "You mean the sum total of energy contained in the universe, the energy that no matter how it is distributed can never grow less."

"Yes."

"I don't quite follow you. We know of course that the entropy of any universe is constantly heading to an even distribution, by that we mean that there will come a time when each and every atom will contain exactly the same amount of energy. In such a case explosives would be unknown, atomic power, solar heat and light. All energy would be evenly spread and it would be impossible for the transference of power. Just as it would be impossible to operate a hydro-electric power station in the middle of an ocean, there must be different levels of water for such a station to work, and so there must be different levels of energy for any transference of power." He stared at Kleon.

"Is that what you mean?"

"In a way, yes."

"Then how can that help us? The old man shook his head. "I have worked on sub-spatial tensors all my life, and I tell you this. It is beyond the power of man to halt the relentless march of entropy, the universe has only a limited amount of power, it can never grow less but it can be so evenly distributed that as far as men are concerned it will be valueless."

"Like a man with a pile of logs perhaps?" Kleon smiled as he tugged at a box. "He can burn them for heat and light, but in so doing he releases their stored energy. Instead of a pile of wood he will have some carbon, heat, light, and a mess of gases. If it were possible to collect and measure all the emitted radiation and by-products, he would still have the equivalent of a pile of logs, but he can only burn them once, and what he would have would be the equivalent of a heap of ash."

"Exactly."

"Now let us get back to the analogy of a hydro-electric power station. You know how they work of course, water from a high level is used to drive turbines as it falls to a lower. The water isn't really used at all, it merely serves as a carrier for the potential force of gravitation, we still have exactly the same amount of water as we started with, but to restore it to its original level would take more power than generated by its fall."

"Naturally, the law of the conservation of energy determines that."

"Of course, but supposing that it wasn't water we were using. Suppose that it were possible to tap the inexhaustible energy of one of the other multiple universes, one with a higher entropy than our own. What then?"

"I see." Hermitage drew in his breath with a soft hiss startlingly loud in the silence of the ship. Jarl moved a box, the soft thud as it dropped to the metal floor plates echoing for a moment before dying away. Kleon nodded.

"So, you follow me. Good. The idea isn't a particularly new one, I read it in an old book when I was studying for my captain's certificate, but those old scientists didn't have our knowledge of sub-space tensors, and to them it was merely an interesting theory. It could be the saving of our civilisation."

"If it worked, but are you certain that it could be done?"

"I am." Kleon looked at the silent figure of the fat engineer. "Tell him, Jarl."

"It happened on our last ship. I was the engineer, and Kleon was my captain. He wanted to try something, and he asked my help, it was something to do with the power room of the ship, and together we built some apparatus, apparatus such as I had never seen before. We activated it somewhere between Earth and Luna—and wrecked the ship!"

"Yes." Kleon looked directly at the old man. "We wrecked the vessel, and for that both Jarl and I were sentenced to death, a sentence later altered to life imprisonment on Mercury, the rest you know."

"You wrecked the ship you say, but doesn't that prove that your invention is unworkable?"

"No!" The fat engineer threw down the last of a coil of wire and strode closer to the old man. "It did work, maybe only for a fraction of time, a micro-second, but it did work. I could see the equipment melting, as energy began to flood through the orifice, tremendous energy which seared the insulation, warped the main drive focusing coils, and exploded into searing destruction. We wrecked the ship, I'll admit that, but the loss was nothing when compared to the gain." He twisted his lips in disgust.

"Landris was too old, too scared of his high position to do other than what he did."

"I see." Hermitage sighed and ran his thin fingers through his white hair. "You escaped in the lifeboats of course, but what of the rest of the crew?"

"I had taken elementary precautions; the crew were left behind at Tycho Station." Kleon grinned. "I'm not complaining about our treatment, I took a chance and lost my gamble, but I am still certain that my invention would work."

"Perhaps. It sounds logical but what method did you use?"

"I based it on the operation of the nulgrav field." He smiled at the old man's sudden start of amazement. "I am one of the few men who can understand the theory, I was always good at that kind of thing, the professors at the space academy used to tell me that I was in some respects a prodigy, I could sense the meaning of abstract mathematical equations much better than most. It seemed to me that if we could but open a door between our own universe and one with a higher entropy level, then power would come flooding through that opening just as water would flood through a hole in the bottom of a container."

He gestured around at the littered equipment.

"I saw it as a succession of energy levels, as though the multiple universes were as a ranked tier of containers, a flight of steps, each step representing a universe, some above our own, and some below. The higher they were, the greater their entropy, and it seemed a simple conclusion to somehow force an opening between our own universe and that of another higher on the energy scale."

"A simple analogy, but a workable one," agreed the old man. "You tried a space-warp of course, a dimensional rending of the sub-etheric continuum?"

"Yes. I constructed an involved apparatus based on the principles of the nulgrav field. I forced power into a closed feedback system, tremendous power; all the power available, as I remember it was five million ergs on the new scale. The power could not dissipate, it created a sub-etheric condition of strain, and by so doing forced a paradox. Logically it could not exist, not when opposed by natural law. It was a self-contained dimensional space-warp, and as such was prevented from forming by the natural laws of our space-time continuum. It could not exist—but it did, and so it had to go somewhere else."

"Naturally. It went to a place or a dimension where it could, it could do nothing else." Hermitage nodded understandingly. "Paradox cannot be allowed in the normal universe, such a field could be created but it was, and so it had to leave the normal continuum for one in which it presented no paradox." He glanced at the tall young captain.

"Now I understand. It went to one of the multiple universes, but as it depended on your apparatus for its continued existence, a bridge was formed. A connection had been made between the two universes, an opening through which power could flow, either from the new universe to our own, or the other way."

He frowned as he thought about it.

"You were lucky, if the bridge had been formed between you and a lower energy level universe, every erg of power would have been drained through the apparatus into that low-entropy plane. In time it would have robbed us of all our energy."

"I thought of that, and the danger was strictly limited. You forget that with the draining of our power the field would have collapsed, and the bridge broken. It was a chance, but one I had to take, in a way I was lucky."

"Naturally, I had not thought of that." Hermitage rubbed his white hair. "Which of the sub-spatial tensors did you use?"

"Le Farge's."

"I see." Hermitage pulled a rumpled mass of paper from a pocket and squatting down on a box began to scribble swift equations.

"What power flow was needed? How long did the field take to form? Did you insulate or isolate the generator?" He rapped swift questions, his thin fingers moving quickly over the paper as he drew strange mathematical symbols and strings of equations. Kleon leaned over him, explaining the fine details of his theory, and correcting the old man when he appeared to wander into speculative realms.

Jarl grunted as he watched, then losing interest in something he could not understand, began to clear away the sorted equipment. From the engine room he brought long lengths of thick cable, connecting them to the remaining ranks of charged accumulators, and running them through a compact power board. He activated the portable welding plant, and working from memory of the earlier machine, began to construct a strong framework of struts and braces. He welded them to the structures of the ship, and gradually order began to grow out of chaos. Kleon glanced at him, then grinned and left the old man to his scribbling. Together the young captain and the fat engineer worked with the stabbing flame of the portable welding plant, the assorted rods of soft almost chemically pure iron, and the glittering lengths of naked silver wire.

Something began to take shape in the centre of the room. Something glittering with silver and quartz, dull with iron and the stripped power leads. Delicate fabrications of glass and metal were supported in a large cradle of strong metal, and the humped bulk of the Le Farge generator was bolted to the floor plates.

"Better make it strong," grunted Jarl. "We may have to move in a hurry, and some of this stuff's too delicate to even breathe on." He stared at a three-foot ball of crystal filled with the glitter of electrodes and grids, droplets of mercury and the dull grey of iron. "Is this vacuum hard?"

"Yes. When activated the hot elements will absorb any surplus gases." Kleon glanced about the growing mass of apparatus. "Better have the orifice a little more towards the hull, we don't want the same trouble as last time."

"We won't," promised the fat engineer. "I've stripped all the cables so that we can't burn the insulation, and there isn't anything inflammable in here. I've lined the area with power collectors and connected the cables to the empty accumulators. I've connected every erg of power in the ship to the output board and fastened dampeners in case of a flare-back." He hesitated, tugging at the lobe of his ear.

"How about radiation?"

"We'll use baffle plates, but I doubt if radiation will trouble us too much. The last time it seemed to be sheer heat and electrical energy, at least what we saw of it was." He glanced at the crouched figure of the old man.

"Better seal this section of the ship. We'll work in space suits, and in case of trouble we can divert the focus of power out of the hull and into space." He nodded as he stared at the equipment. "Better have a quick-release air valve fitted to the lull. If the apparatus starts to short over an air-gap, we can evacuate this section and work in vacuum."

"Wait!" Hermitage scrambled to his feet, his eyes burning in the thin whiteness of his lined features.

"I've been working on some figures, and I don't like what they tell me."

"What do you mean?"

"This proposed release of power from a high-entropy level universe, it can be dangerous, Kleon. Too dangerous!"

"No! I told you that if the power began to drain from the ship into a low-entropy level universe the power generating the communication field would collapse and the drain stopped. The same would happen if too much power came through, the apparatus would be destroyed, and the bridge broken." Impatiently the tall young captain turned to his work, the sharp flame from the portable welder limning the harsh lines of his features.

"You must listen!" Hermitage grabbed at the young man's arm, spinning him around with unexpected strength, Kleon sighed and lifted the opaque eye-shield covering his cold grey eyes.

"Well?"

"You are right, but only up to a point. If the power began to drain, then as you say the field would collapse, but it doesn't work both ways."

"It must do, logically it can't do anything else."

"Logic!" The old man glared his contempt. "What have we to do with logic? Logically the field couldn't exist, but it does, so how far can we depend on logic?" He shook his white head.

"No, Kleon. I have found a great danger. Listen. If we open a bridge between our own universe and one of too high an entropy level, then the energy of that plane will come blasting through in a torrent of utter destruction." He paused his eyes tense and worried.

"Imagine what would happen then. A point would have been created, a point of searing energy. A new star would blossom into space, an expanding star, and we should be atomic dust burnt to ash by the fury of our own creation!"

"What of it?" Kleon shrugged as he returned to his work. "Maybe that's how stars were created, by a break-through from one universe to another. Weak points in the continuum, a tearing of the space-time barriers between one level and another." He smiled at the old man. "We must take that chance."

"We dare not." Hermitage slumped tiredly onto a packing box. "If we are just a trifle out in our calculations, we may doom our universe to a burning death. If I am right and we do hit too high an energy level, then the expanding star which we will have created will swell until it fills the galaxy with searing energy. Life will vanish, the planets will rotate as charred embers in a sea of universal flame."

Kleon shrugged, then looked at Jarl. Slowly he removed the opaque eye-shield and put down the lightless welder. "Come on," he ordered, then stiffened with shocked surprise.

The ship rang to the sudden clangour of alarms.

CHAPTER TEN

Branson met them as they climbed to the top of the stairs leading to the control room. The big man trembled with excitement, his fiery red hair bristling like a halo around his broad features. He jerked a thumb at the flaring visi-screen.

"A ship! Headed this way and coming fast."

"Any recognition?" Kleon grabbed at the big man's arm.

"No. I didn't wait to scan them, but who else could it be but the Guard? That trader must have sold us out."

"I doubt it." Kleon stared at the swelling shape on the screen. Fire spat from swelling venturis at the rear of the sturdy craft, and the menacing curves of gun turrets showed clearly on the flaring view plate.

"They probably learned there was something happening from the agent." He sprang towards the control chair snapping quick orders.

"Jarl, get down to the engines. Branson, you get to the turret but hold your fire. Hermitage, sit here with me."

Tensely he sat staring at the swiftly approaching vessel narrowing his eyes at the sleek lines of the strange craft. It wasn't a starship, but that meant little. It could have been a private vessel, a ship belonging to some inter-planet trader but such vessels were few and rarely found within atmosphere. He stared at the nearing shape, trying to spot the recognition signals blazoned on the hull.

Abruptly the radio crackled into strident life, and Kleon activated the speaker on the board before him.

"Starship, ahoy! Starship, ahoy! Do not blast. Do not blast. Stand by to receive boarders."

Kleon smiled tightly as he heard the well-remembered hailing code and leaned close to the speaker of his own radio.

"You are spotted," he snapped crisply. "Identify yourselves."

"Interplanetary Guard calling," echoed the radio. "Stand by to receive borders."

"Identify yourselves!" Kleon stabbed the panel before him. "Starship XL 113 Sol 3 here. Who are you?"

"Interplanetary Guard calling," repeated the radio. "If you blast, we'll open fire."

Abruptly the tall young captain cut the radio and stabbed at the intercom buttons.

"Control to engine. Jarl, feed power to the main drive."

"Engine to control. Ready to blast within five seconds."

"Good." Kleon threw another switch.

"Control to turret. Open fire on strange vessel when in range. Fire at will."

"Right!" Branson chuckled as he answered the command. Hermitage looked doubtfully at the captain.

"Must we?" After all they are the Guard."

"No." Kleon shook his head. "That ship isn't a Guard vessel, probably some power pirates or hijackers come to see what they can steal. They didn't answer the recognition signal correctly, a Guard ship would always do that."

Impatiently, he watched the swinging hand of the chronometer before him.

"Control to engine. Stand by to blast."

"Ready."

"Then here we go!" Slowly Kleon depressed a lever before him, and deep within the ship a giant muttered to sudden life.

Flame spouted from the gaping mouths of the great venturis, the vivid blue-white flame of streaming ions fed from the raging heart of an atomic pile. The thunder of the rockets swelled, grew into a roaring whistle, and slowly the great ship began to rise on a pillar of fire.

Beneath them the vegetation smoked and burst into flame from the heat of their exhaust, and the fierce heat of the rocket blast baked the soft loam into cracked and steaming ruin. Higher they mounted, higher, and slowly the weight of acceleration pressure began to force them deep into their padded chairs.

The radio crackled with a sudden desperate urgency, and on the flaring view plate of the visi-screen, the strange ship seemed to veer as it aligned the menacing barrels of its guns to the starship.

"Cease blasting! Cease or we fire!"

Kleon ignored the peremptory command, instead he threw the switch of the intercom.

"Control to turret. Open fire at will!"

Branson chuckled. "Watch," he invited. "I'm good at this."

From the approaching ship fire suddenly spat from one of the turrets, a pulsing stream of searing energy stabbing directly towards the slender shape of the starship. A second turret opened fire, and the atmosphere glared to the released energy.

"Your last chance," warned the radio. "Cease blasting or we'll fuse your venturis."

Kleon thinned his lips as he fought to keep the rising vessel on an even balance. He narrowed his eyes at the tracking shape of the strange vessel and fed more power to the thundering rockets.

Fire spouted from the turrets of the menacing ship, vivid bolts of electrical destruction. They flared towards the flaming venturis—and abruptly Branson answered back!

The multiple guns of the single turret snarled as they hurled their stabbing tongues of searing energy at the smaller vessel. A turret burst into molten ruin, and a portion of the hull glowed red as it tried to absorb the flaming energy of the starship's guns. Desperately the strange ship veered, blasting away from certain destruction, and as it went it fired every weapon bearing on its target.

The starship reeled, lurching as the thundering bolts smashed against the hull throwing the rising vessel off balance and filling the hull with the hot smell of burnt metal. Kleon tensed in the padded chair as his hands flickered across the controls, making delicate adjustments of the steering tubes, feeding power to the whining gyroscopes, fighting to restore balance to the starship.

Dimly he became aware of the snarling thunder of their own weapons. Once! Twice! A third time, and in the flickering surface of the visi-screen something exploded, blossoming into a fierce gout of blue-white fire. Slowly he fought the ship back onto an even balance, and wiped sweat from his face and neck.

"Got them!" He smiled with grim satisfaction as he watched the plunging ruin of what had once been a trim vessel. Impatiently, he thumbed the buttons of the intercom.

"Control to engine."

"What damage, Jarl?"

"Nothing serious, their guns were too weak to do more than melt a fin and fuse a section of the hull."

"Good. Stand by the engines." Kleon pressed another button. "Control to turret."

"Yes?"

"What kept you so long? They took three shots at us before you replied, I thought that you were a trained gunner."

"I couldn't help it, Kleon. Their shots threw the ship off balance and spoiled my aim. I wanted to conserve what power we had, and that meant making each shot count."

"Never mind now, you got them anyway." He leaned back in the padded chair as the acceleration pressure began to mount beneath the mighty thrust of the thundering venturis.

Higher they climbed, higher, the atmosphere shrilling about the smooth hull warming it by sheer friction caused by the speed of their passage. The shrilling died, faded to a thin whisper and vanished as the stars shone bright and clear against the black velvet of space.

"Now to work." Kleon adjusted the firing levers setting them so that the acceleration pressure, equalled one-half Earth gravity. "We must be quick, this acceleration uses too much fuel but we can't work in free fall, and landing would use as much fuel with the danger of fresh attack."

"Are we heading for Earth?" Hermitage rose thankfully from his chair and stared at the glittering glory of the naked stars.

"No. We haven't enough fuel ever to reach it, even if we had the power to activate the nulgrav field." Kleon made an adjustment to the controls staring intently at the singing needle of a dial. "I've thrown us into an orbit around the sun. At an acceleration of sixteen feet per second per second we shouldn't be too uncomfortable, and half a grav acceleration is better than none." He smiled at the old man.

"You had better check your figures on the computer while Branson and Jarl work with me finishing the apparatus. I must check the hull, those shots may have weakened something. Let me know what you find, I'll be either in the engine room or working on the entropy field."

He clattered down the stairs as the old man bent over the computer, setting up endless sets of equations and frowning at his scribbled notes.

Branson had already reached the lower levels and he frowned at the assembled mass of strange equipment almost covering the entire section above the engine room. He glanced up as Kleon entered the room and gestured towards the apparatus.

"Is this the great invention?"

"Part of it, the rest is a complex mathematical equation impossible to duplicate." The tall young captain smiled at the puzzled expression on the big man's broad features. "By that I mean that it wouldn't do anyone any good to steal this machine, its operation depends more on the correct flow of power than the actual coils themselves."

"Why tell me that?" Branson stared at the lithe figure before him. "Did you think that I intended stealing the invention?" He laughed curtly as he stared about him. "I hope that you're satisfied, we could all have lived rich for the rest of our lives on what this junk has cost." He stopped and examined the humped bulk of the Le Farge generator. "I'll bet this alone took more power than we can spare."

"It took a little," admitted Kleon quietly. "In fact if we don't succeed in getting more power soon we shall have to head for a planet and ground the ship." He shrugged at the expression on the redhead's face and picked up the eye-shield and welding plant.

"Stay here if you want to, Jarl will tell you what to do, but don't touch anything, and stay out of my way."

"I'll stay, after all we're in this together, win or lose." He grinned and held out his hand. "Forget it, Kleon, I may have flown off the handle a little, but think nothing of it. Friend?" Kleon took the proffered hand.

"Friends," he said, and smiled. Together they bent to their work.

"The whole trick is forming a closed feed-back system within the area of an orifice through which we hope the captured power will stream," explained Kleon. "We obviously can't have any equipment within that area, if we did it would be destroyed, and the field would collapse as soon as created."

"I see." Branson stared at the intricate coils of soft iron. "I suppose that you generate a terrific magnetic field within the area, a closed field held by the magnetic flux?"

"Yes. The idea is an old one, but we have carried it a step further. The magnetic field will guide the electronic stream in a circular orbit, we feed power into that orbit, tremendous power at incredible voltages, and the result will be a sub-etheric condition of dimensional stress. Normally nothing would happen but some interesting phenomena, but we are using a spherical force field, and we are not using normal electricity."

"Then what are you using?"

"Mesotrons."

"I don't understand?" Branson looked up from where he held a twisted coil of dull iron. "Electricity is a normal flow of electrons from one pole to another, we have used it for more than a thousand years, what other force can you use?"

"I told you, mesotrons." Kleon smiled at the puzzled expression on the big man's broad features. "That is why we had to have a Le Farge generator. It converts normal electricity into mesotronic current. A mesotron is a subatomic particle with a mass about one hundred and fifty time as great but with the same charge as that of an electron. The result is that we can get a tremendous mass via kinetic energy."

"Now I begin to see it." The redhead wiped sweat from his broad face. "You feed that current into a closed feed-back spherical force field. The mesotrons are speeded by the magnetic field and with their increased mass naturally they tend to implode. The result...?" He grinned. "Now understand, Kleon, why didn't you explain all this to Earth scientists?"

"I did, they laughed at me." Memory darkened the harsh features of the tall adventurer. "They said that I didn't know what I was talking about, that I was too young to know anything about the subject." He shrugged. "I tried to convince them, tried too hard, and when they finally refused to let me speak about it anymore, I went ahead on my own."

"Is that what sent you to Mercury?"

"Yes."

"What about Jarl, was he in it too?"

"He was my engineer, he helped me assemble the apparatus, and insisted on sharing the blame." He looked up as the fat engineer entered the room. "Everything ready, Jarl?"

"Yes." The fat man slumped down on to the edge of a supporting strut. "I did what I could, we can turn every erg of power into the field, and I have built cut-outs in case we hit the wrong energy level." He blinked tiredly at the intricate coils and glittering glass and crystal. "We haven't too much power, Kleon, not nearly enough to experiment. Unless we can tap a high-entropy level and store the power we may be in trouble."

"Cheer up." Kleon slapped the engineer on the back and straightened his aching body. "We are all tired, too much work and not enough food. Branson, how about you getting us all some food? You'll find thermocans in the galley, and some vitaminised coffee."

"Certainly." The big redhead threw down his tools and rubbed the back of his neck. "We must have been working longer than we realised. I could do with a week's sleep and a seven-course dinner. My brain's as tired as my body."

"Get the food," ordered Kleon. "While you're about it tell the old man to come down here, we are all in this together."

While waiting for the big man to return with the thermocans, Kleon crossed to the medical cabinet and took out a small phial. He shook out four green tablets, then hesitated for a moment looking down at his hand. He shrugged and spilled a further four tablets into his palm and looked up as Branson and Hermitage entered the room.

"Here," he held out two of the tablets to each man, "take these with the coffee."

"What are they?"

"Anti-fatigue pills, they will freshen our minds and bodies. It wouldn't do for us to make any sort of a mistake now."

Hermitage looked up from where he sipped his warmed energised soup, his eyes were red with too much concentration and his old, lined features were strained with worry.

"Is it finished then?"

Kleon nodded, and together they stared at the machine which could bring new life to a power-starved civilisation.

CHAPTER ELEVEN

The suits were harsh, and the rough fabric chafed tender skin, but excitement made the purely physical discomforts of secondary importance. Kleon worked his fingers within the fabric of his gloves and wished that he dared leave them off, then smiled as he remembered what would happen to them if he did.

Before him rose the power board connected to the gleaming mass of intricate apparatus assembled in the centre of the chamber. Overhead fluorescent lighting limned the glittering quartz and crystal with little halos of shimmering light, contrasting strangely with the dull sheen of almost pure iron and the bright sparkle of naked silver.

Bulbous in their space suits, the face plates open but ready to be swung shut by any fall in atmospheric pressure, they stood around the edges of the writhing coils watching the vacant orifice in the centre. Jarl, seeming even more fat and shapeless in his suit. Branson, his big bulk swelling the thick fabric and metal, contrasting oddly with the old professor almost lost in his too-big protective clothing. Kleon watched them for a moment, then gave last-second instructions.

"You all know what to do. Jarl will watch the power and Hermitage will check the sub-spatial tensors. If the machinery begins to short across an air-gap, Branson will immediately evacuate the chamber. It's sealed from the rest of the ship except the engine room, and we can afford to lose the air. Any questions?"

"What happens when the power begins coming through?" Branson licked his lips as he stared at the empty orifice.

"Jarl, Hermitage and myself will take care of that. You just concentrate on helping where you can, and staying out of the way where you can't." He smiled at the big man. "I know that you want to do what you can, but this is a job for experts. When we have another ship to blast out of space, we'll take orders from you, but until then each man to his own trade." He glanced at the board before him.

"We'll communicate by helmet radio if we have to, but not unless it is essential. Any other questions? No? Then here we go!"

His gloved hands darted over the board before him, and power began quivering through the looming machine.

It began as the faintest trembling, climbing to a shrilling scream as the surging pressure of the mesotrons increased. A shimmering grew around the writhing coils, an eye-twisting ripple of transient light clinging to the dull iron of the involuted coils and flowing as if it were water along the supporting stanchions.

Kleon manipulated the controls, biting his lips as he watched needles climb and fall on the instruments before him denoting the drain of power from the ranked accumulators. The shrilling scream climbed yet higher, vanishing as a thin ghost of a sound as it climbed into the inaudible supersonic range beyond human hearing. Pain stabbed at them as the sound reached a harmonic resonating to the structure of bone itself, stabbed and vanished as the vibrations soared to even higher levels.

Something seemed to grow in the circular space at the heart of the machine. A mist, twisting and writhing in the grip of strange powers and the surging force of spinning mesotrons. It grew, filling the entire space with a straining mass of subatomic particles guided and speeded by the tremendous force of the external magnetic field.

Kleon threw yet more power into the humming generator, then yet more, forcing still more of the heavy particles within the confines of the closed field. Tensely he waited by the power board his eyes flickering between the surging cloud of mist and the tell-tale needles of his instrument dials.

Tension grew within the room, the tension of surging eddy currents, and the tension of overstrained emotions. With startling abruptness, the coiling globe of mist vanished. It disappeared, flung into some alien dimension by the inexorable force of natural law. It quivered, writhed beneath the impact of irresistible forces, and was gone.

Power whined from the humming generator, was sucked from the ranked accumulators, was drained from the very lights and instruments themselves. Frost glittered on the machines, sparkling from the dull iron coils, and a thick white rime coated the metal of walls and hull. It grew cold, terribly cold, cold with the icy grip of outer space, so cold that it seemed as if the very air would solidify.

Kleon jerked forward, cutting switches with a sweep of his arm, and the dull report of breaking cut-outs echoed through the chamber. The machines whined to a stop, the power ceased to flow through the thick cables, and heat slowly returned to the frigid chamber.

Kleon leaned against the frost covered power board and stared dully at the silent machines. Branson shivered and swung his gloved hands together.

"What happened?" His breath coiled in thick white plumes on the frigid air. He frowned at the rime coated walls. "Didn't it work?"

"It worked," said Kleon grimly. He stared at the little figure of the old professor. "We must have hit a low-entropy level, our power and energy just drained through the orifice." He shivered and glanced at the instrument dials. "That just about does it."

"What do you mean?" The old professor squinted at the ranked dials, his eyes red and sore-looking beneath the thin white hair of his brows.

"We are almost out of power." Kleon gestured towards the instrument dials. "It took more power than I thought, the field simply drank it. When we opened a bridge that power and quite a lot more drained through." He sighed, his shoulders slumping with weariness and loss of hope. "I'm afraid that our gamble is over—we've lost."

"No!" Hermitage squinted at the power board. "Perhaps not."

"What do you mean?"

"I did quite a bit of figuring while you were building this machine and I believe that I can solve our problem." He smiled at the incredulous expression on the young captain's harsh features.

"Look at it this way. If you wanted to shift a heavy weight you can do it either of two ways. You can move it by brute strength, or you can move it by applied science, leverage. Now do you begin to understand?"

"Yes." Kleon straightened himself from the panel. "Can it be done?"

"I think, yes. Up to now you have been trying to open a passage between two universes, and you have done it by using brute strength, sheer power. It need not necessarily be the correct way."

"Then what do you suggest?"

"A subtle difference in our use of power." He shivered a little and glanced at Branson. "Could we perhaps have some hot coffee? That drain of power chilled me, and I think better when warm."

The big man nodded, and leaving the chamber returned with several thermocans. He thrust in the tops and swirled one in his gloved hand waiting for the drink to warm.

"You think that we still have a chance?"

Hermitage nodded, sipping at the hot sweet coffee. Jarl joined them, his fat features twisted with worry. Glumly he accepted one of the thermocans.

"We're low on power, Kleon. Too low. We shall have to head for a planet if we ever intend landing this ship, either that or cut the rocket drive."

"We can't work in free fall." Kleon stared at the shivering figure of the old professor. "How long will it take for you to work out the new equations?"

"I've already done it." Hermitage set down his empty can and rummaged in the outer pocket of his space suit. "Your theory is perfect as far as it goes, Kleon, but I have had a lifetime's training on the subtleties of the sub-spatial tensors, and I believe that I have found the determining factor." He drew a stylo from his pocket and began to scribble a string of mathematical symbols.

"Now if we take the sign alpha to be the power factor, the sign beta to be the directional force, and the sign gamma to be the resistant, you can see what would happen when we alter them—so."

"It might work," mused Kleon staring at the symbols, "and if we altered the pi factor it should be possible to choose any entropy level we determine." He smiled at the old man. "I was worried about that," he admitted. "It was too much like stabbing in the dark, but there was nothing I could think of to avoid it." He clenched one fist and slammed it down on his knee.

"If only those fools on Earth had listened to me! With the resources of the scientists, we could have solved these factors long ago." He smiled and shrugged. "Well, it's no good crying over spilt milk. You realise that unless we succeed this time there'll be no second attempt. Even with the reduced power requirements of your new sub-etheric tensors, it means almost draining the ship." He stared at the intent features of the two other men.

"Which shall it be? Do we stay here and have one more try, or do we return to one of the planets and abandon the ship?

If we stay and fail, then we shall not be able to land. It means death, death for all of us."

"What have we to lose?" Branson grinned and slapped the fat engineer on the back. "I say have another go, we're ruined either way, and I'd rather have a clean death than rot on a labour squad."

"How about you, Jarl?"

"I'll stay."

"Good." Kleon moved towards the power board. "To work then. Ready?"

They nodded, their eyes bright and eager. Hermitage joined the tall figure of the young adventurer, and together they made the necessary adjustments.

"Now!" Kleon activated the controls and stood waiting as the murmur of surging power echoed through the chamber.

Slowly the field began to form, the dull iron of the enfolding coils to shimmer with the induced radiance of pulsing magnetic eddy currents. Mist swirled within the opening of the orifice, a coiling writhing grey-white mist, humming a little as it built up mass and mesotronic charge.

Kleon blinked as he looked at it. It seemed different, a subtle alteration in the shape and direction of coiling. He glanced at the dials of his instruments and nodded with satisfaction as he noted the reduced power needs of the created field. He stared at the eye-twisting mist pulsing in the open orifice at the heart of the machine then stepped up the power a little. Needles swung on a row of dials, and automatically he threw in a fresh series of accumulators, the last. He tightened his lips as he stared at the core of the assembled apparatus. If they failed—

They did not fail!

Heat streamed with sudden abruptness from the heart of the machine. Heat and pouring radiance flooding the chamber with searing brilliance. Hermitage cried out and staggered back his hands pressed to his eyes. Jarl yelled as he lunged forward and worked frantically at the bulk surrounding of machines. Kleon smiled and adjusted the controls of the power board.

"We did it!" Branson stood staring at the glittering splendour of the streaming power, his eyes screwed and streaming with tears as he stared. "Look! Power! A million ergs of power, and all ours. All ours!"

"Quick!" Jarl staggered back from the miniature sun. "Help me, Kleon, the thermocouples!"

Desperately they sweated over the power-gathering instruments, straining to save and store some of the flood of power pouring through the orifice at the heart of the machine. Irritably Branson stripped off his space suit and bent to work beside them, his half-naked torso glistening with sweat. Hermitage staggered back and slumped unconscious at the foot of the stairs, and Jarl gasped and wheezed as he strained at the heavy bulks of his machines.

"Enough!" Kleon staggered to his feet, his eyes red and sore. "The radiation and heat, we've got to get out of here!" Stooping, he swung the limp figure of the old man to his shoulder and staggered towards the stairs.

"Branson! Jarl! Get out of here!"

Together they forced open the door and gasped with relief at the relatively cool air of the upper parts of the starship. Kleon grunted as he kicked the door shut and gestured towards the control room.

"Quick, Upstairs, I think that the old man has been burnt by the radiation."

He glanced at Branson and frowned at the ugly red blotches marring his white torso. "You should have retained the space suit," he snapped. "Look at your chest."

The big redhead shrugged as he glanced down at the ugly red marks. "I've been sunburnt before," he said casually. "I'll live."

"Let's hope so." Gently he lowered the limp figure of the old man to the metal floor and began stripping off the thick suit. "Jarl. Get some anti-radiation shots from the medical cabinet, some salve and a nerve block, give them to Red here."

"Treat the old man first." Branson bit his lips against a sudden tide of agony from his seared chest. "I can wait." Jarl grunted and slid the needle of a hypodermic into the great vein of the big man's arm. As he pressed the plunger the scintillant blue fluid flowed steadily into Branson's bloodstream, bringing instant relief from pain as the fluid blocked all sensations from the damaged nerves.

"I've not finished yet," said the fat engineer. He reloaded the hypodermic and emptied it at several points on the big man's chest and arms. "We don't want you sick with radiant poisoning. Here!" He threw a container of salve towards the redhead. "Smear this on, smear it thick, it will restore the damaged skin cells. I'll spray you with a hormone quick-healing plastic dressing later." He looked towards the silent figure of the old man.

"How is he, Kleon?"

"Bad." The tall young adventurer rose from where he had knelt beside the old man. Slowly he stripped off his suit. "His eyes are gone, Jarl. He must have been blinded with the unshielded radiation when the bridge was first formed. His face is burnt, but that isn't too important, we can heal that." He stood looking thoughtfully down at the unconscious figure. Branson crossed the room and stood beside him, rubbing his raw chest with the salve.

"What shall we do now?"

"Give him anti-radiation shots, a nerve block to stop the pain, and a hormone spray for quick healing. What more can we do?"

"How about his eyes?"

"They're gone. We can't graft new ones, and we're too far from a body bank to arrange for the operation." Kleon frowned down at the limp figure of the old man. "We'll do what we can. He must wait until we reach a hospital to regain his sight. We can save him pain and heal his face, but that's all we can do."

"If we reach a hospital." Jarl pointed to an instrument, the slender needle of which rested far into the red danger area. "Look at the thermometer! Unless we can bring that miniature sun beneath control, we'll fuse the entire lower portion of the ship. What can we do about it, Kleon?"

"How much power have we now?"

"A little, the thermocouples are recharging the accumulators. Why?"

"The only way to control the power point is to divert some of the energy outside the hull. We can restrict the orifice, but that would only serve to narrow the beam." He snapped his fingers at a sudden thought. "Jarl! Can we shift the orifice so that the beam itself will serve as a means of powering the ionic drive?"

"Maybe." The engineer frowned in thought. "I could alter the lay-out of the engine room a little. We have some reflector shields, ninety-nine percent effective, they should serve to deflect the radiation." He looked up at the tall figure of his captain. "I think we could just about do it."

"Good." Kleon spun to face the redhead. "Branson! You stay here and look after the old man, you know what to do. If he recovers consciousness tell him what we are trying to do, he may have an answer to the problem." He laughed curtly. "One day we'll be satisfied, first we haven't enough power, and now we have too much. Ready, Jarl?"

"Yes."

"Then to work."

Together they left the control room, each carrying the bulk of a space suit as they clattered down the stairs.

Heat lashed at them two levels down. A lung-drying heat, seeming to blister their skin and sear their eyes with unsuspected radiation. Kleon paused and began to don the thick fabric of the space suit. Jarl followed his example.

"We could do with some of those suits we used on the Solar Expedition," he grumbled as they fastened the airtight seals. "Remember that, Kleon? Triple vacuum insulation and anti-radiation shielding proof against almost anything." He fastened his face plate and spoke through the suit radio. "What's the plan, captain?"

"Get into the room and evacuate it. We'll have to work in the suits anyway, and we may as well cut down the heat transference to the rest of the ship." He paused just before the door. "Take no chances, Jarl. We have enough power now to land the ship, and we can always try again."

"Can we?" The fat engineer sounded dubious. "The last time we tried to get official support we wound up on Mercury. Let's not chance that again."

Kleon laughed and rested his hand on the door. "Ready?"

"Ready." Swiftly the tall captain threw open the door and slammed it fast behind them.

A sun glowed in the centre of the room. A scintillating point of utter brilliance radiating heat and light from amid the shadowy shapes of assembled apparatus. Kleon glanced worriedly at the dully glowing iron coils, now at red heat and beginning to soften from their original position. Quickly he crossed the room and spun the quick-release air valve.

A thin whining whispered around his suit, a faint whistle of rushing air, and as it died, the fabric of the space suit stiffened from internal air pressure. The hot iron dulled several degrees as it lost some of its heat from the rapid expansion of air, and the room cleared of heat haze and released gases.

Swiftly the two men set to work. Baffles of almost perfectly reflecting alloy were welded into position; the floor plates were cut and several engines slid along their carriages to fresh positions. Jarl hovered about his precious recharging equipment, connecting fresh ranks of accumulators to the throbbing surge of power flooding from the centre of the entropy field equipment, and Kleon delicately tried various adjustments of power as he tried to stem the too-great flood of raw energy.

Slowly order grew out of chaos. Slowly the throbbing flood of power ceased to be a danger, channelled and directed away from the metal of the hull and allowed to dissipate into space. Wearily they stood and watched the searing golden tide of energy, then half numb with utter fatigue, they returned to the control room.

Branson met them as they staggered into the instrument-lined room, his features twisted with emotion as he helped them doff the heavy suits.

"How did it go?" He stared at them, his eyes glittering with excitement. "Did you manage to control the power?"

"Yes." Kleon almost fell into a chair and relaxed his aching body. Slowly he straightened, his eyes hard and cold as they stared at the gun pointing directly at his stomach.

CHAPTER TWELVE

Branson grinned and gestured with the weapon. "Sit still," he warned. He turned the squat barrel to include the fat engineer. "That means you too! Do as I say and you won't get hurt."

"Just what do you think that you're doing?" Kleon stared coldly at the big redhead. "Have you gone out of your mind?"

"No." Branson smiled, his white teeth gleaming in the indirect lighting. "I think it is time that we made a few changes. I've taken orders from you long enough, now it's your turn. If you do as I say and do it quick, I may let you live, but don't make the mistake of thinking that I can't do without you."

"What do you want?"

"I want to know what you intend doing with your discovery. Are you going to sell it to the highest bidder, or what?"

"That's my business."

"No! That's just what it isn't. I have a share in this, and I want to know. Well? Do you tell me or do I make my own conclusions?"

Kleon yawned and slumped back into the padded comfort of the control chair. He glanced towards the limp figure of the professor, his face glistening beneath a newly-applied hormone spray. He nodded towards the old man.

"How is he?"

"Resting, I did what I could for him." Branson gestured with the flare gun. "Enough of him, are you going to get sensible?"

"Yes." Cold grey eyes stared at the rumpled halo of red hair. "I intend selling this discovery to the highest bidder." He glanced at the visi-screen. "We are in line with Rigel, and from what I know of the Rigellians they will gladly offer me a planetary empire for what I have within this ship." He smiled at the glowering figure of the big man. "Surprised?"

"No. I thought as much, well you are wrong. I'll tell you what you are going to do with this ship. You are going to take it back to Earth, and I am going with you."

"Are you?" Kleon smiled and suddenly kicked his foot forward in a sharp motion. His metal-soled boot hurled through the air, and before the big man could dodge the missile it had struck him full in the face. He cried out, swinging the heavy barrel of his weapon, then slumped to the metal deck a thin rill of blood pouring from his mouth.

Kleon grinned savagely as he stooped and picked up the weapon. "Fool!" he said contemptuously. "He was too busy looking at my eyes to watch my hands. I never thought that an old spaceman could be taken in by that old trick."

Thoughtfully he rubbed his split knuckles and slumped back in his chair watching the unconscious man. Branson stirred, licked his lips, then sank back to the metal deck plates as he saw the menacing orifice of the squat-barrelled flare-gun.

"Well?"

"Perhaps it is time that we end this farce," suggested Kleon gently. "Who are you?"

"Branson, an ex-navigator on the Mercury power ships, you know that."

"Let me put it this way," suggested Kleon. "*What are you?*"

"What do you mean?" Branson licked his lips again and stared at the weapon pointing at his middle. "I don't understand you?"

"Don't you?" Kleon smiled without humour, and suddenly struck with the heavy barrel of the pistol. The big man snarled with rage, an ugly red weal marring his cheek.

"Well? Are you going to talk or do I pistol-whip you into a shapeless pulp?"

"You wouldn't dare," whispered the big man. "You couldn't, you're not made that way."

"So!" Kleon smiled and relaxed in the padded softness of his chair. "Now we're getting somewhere. You seem to know a little more about me than I thought, far more than you should. Well?"

Branson licked his lips again and stared silently at the menacing weapon. He shook his head, and for a moment his eyes rested hopefully on the silent figure of the fat engineer. Kleon smiled, jiggling the heavy pistol in his hand.

"Catch!" he called and threw the weapon towards Jarl. Numbly the fat man took it, holding it carelessly in one fat paw.

"I never did trust coincidence," murmured the young captain. "Once perhaps, even twice, but more than that no. It was coincidence that both Jarl and myself should be reprieved and sentenced to Mercury instead of death. It was more than coincidence that we should be shipped with men who had a tremendous effect on our actions. An old man who happened to be an expert in sub-spatial tensors. A dark man who didn't have very much to do with us, but who served as a terrible example to Jarl, and an ex-navigator who seemed to know just what to do next." He shook his head in silent mockery.

"Too many coincidences, far too many."

"What are you getting at?" Branson writhed on the hard floor and stared at the fat engineer.

"The escape of course was planned, I would have to be too big a fool not to have seen the obvious, but why? Why were we allowed to steal a ship full of stored power? Myself, my engineer, an old man who knew all about the type of work I was doing, and you, Branson. I can place the rest, but what, are you?"

"You know who I am."

"I know what you say you are, but I don't believe everything I hear." Kleon smiled at his engineer. "Comfortable, Jarl? Good. Don't get careless now." He relaxed even more into his chair.

"Obviously someone was after the secret of entropic power, but who? Earth? They could have had the secret for the asking, it was something I was only too eager to have given away. Rigel? Possible, but how could they have planned the escape so neatly. They could have one man in their pay, perhaps two, but more than two were needed." He leaned forward staring at the man on the floor. "Who was it, Branson? Who arranged all this farce?"

The redhead remained silent, staring at the fat engineer with glittering eyes. Kleon glanced at the visi-screen and turned to the control board. Carefully he read meters and adjusted rheostats, then operated the steering rockets with delicate touches of his slender fingers.

Without any warning he activated the nulgrav drive!

Branson jerked as the familiar tension seized his body, and for a moment he seemed about to attack the fat engineer, then as the flare-gun centred on his chest, he relaxed licking his dry lips.

"Where are we going?"

"To where we can sell the entropic power secret," said Kleon cheerfully. "It may be a long trip, but we have plenty of power now and I'll see that you get your share of what's coming."

He stared at a point just over Branson's head.

"Power," he whispered. "A planetary empire, luxury undreamed of and power unthinkable. I'll rule as no man has ever ruled, and my name will descend to posterity as Kleon the First. Emperor of Space!"

"You're mad!" Branson rose slowly from the metal floor and held out his hand. Silently Jarl handed over the weapon and stepped to the control panel. Kleon watched him, his grey eyes hard and cold.

"You too, Jarl?" He shook his head. "Leave the controls alone!"

"No!" Branson gestured with the heavy weapon. "Reset our course, Jarl, you know to where."

"Leave it!" Kleon surged to his feet and thrust the engineer away. He laughed at the startled expression on the big man's face as he tried to fire the gun. Tried and failed.

"My legs are safe, Branson, I removed the charges before I gave the pistol to my loyal engineer." He didn't trouble to hide his sneer. "What did they offer *you*, Jarl?" He smiled at the expression on the fat man's face.

"Now perhaps we can talk. Who are you, Branson?"

"A psychologist."

"A psychologist?" Kleon shook his head. "I should have known, but how could I guess. Working for Earth I suppose?"

"Yes." Branson slumped into a padded chair. "Try and understand, Kleon, the whole plot was for one purpose and one alone."

"Entropic power?"

"Naturally, but for a little more than that. Landris made an honest mistake, he couldn't know that you were really on the track of a new power source, and before he could guess, you had been sentenced to death." The big man stirred in his chair.

"He was in an awkward position, the balance of power on the World Council is precarious, his enemies are ready and eager to replace him with their own man, a man who would see that power allocations went to his friends. Landris knew that, and so he had to be careful."

"So he changed the sentence to one of life imprisonment on Mercury?"

"Yes, but he did more than that. You were never intended to remain on the hell planet, but you were safe there, and could be watched. Hermitage, Darko and I were shipped with you. Darko wasn't important, but Hermitage was. It was his job to help you discover the secret."

"I guessed that, but what was your job?"

"To ensure that the secret was discovered for Earth." Branson smiled as he stared at the cold grey eyes of the tall young captain. "You are young, and you made no secret of the way you felt when you were sentenced. You were openly contemptuous of the World Council, and Landris has had great experience with men. He knew that you would be resentful, easy prey to anyone offering you what Earth had denied. He sent me with you to make sure that you would not be tempted."

"How?"

"I knew your psychological pattern. I have deliberately forced you to take a certain course of action. The escape was easy, you had been injured rescuing the old man, he took a chance there, but I knew that you would help him. While you were physically at a low ebb, Jarl worked on your emotions with his tale of seeing Darko blinded and insane. That primed you for the arranged escape. The rest you know."

"Not quite, your work didn't end there."

"No," admitted the big man, "it didn't. I have deliberately suggested certain lines of selfish action, knowing that you would go against them." He smiled for the first time since the loss of his weapon.

"You and I have a natural antipathy towards each other, one of those things no one can ever explain. We just don't like each other, a dislike which I have done my best to encourage. Whatever I suggested you would be certain to oppose because of that emotion. Now?" He slumped in his chair. "I am beaten, you have been a little too clever for me."

"You are wrong." Kleon smiled and stared at his engineer. "Strangely I never suspected you, Jarl. I would have sworn that you at least would always have remained loyal to me. What persuaded you?"

"I did." The big man glanced at the fat engineer. "I helped to break that loyalty, but only with the help of an ideal. Jarl is loyal to you, Kleon, but he is more loyal to Earth. He would die for you, but he would suffer hell itself for the planet of his birth. Power doesn't interest him, money, wealth, the dreams of conquest all fade into insignificance beside the one true reality. Earth!"

"Do you think that I am to be bought and sold?" Kleon rose from his chair and stared at the swirling stars mirrored on the smooth surface of the visi-screen.

"Do you think that Earth means nothing to me? Why do you think I invented this new power source? To gain wealth? No. It was something which the old man said which decided me. Up to that time I will admit that I had no great love for Earth. The dead weight of old men's hands rested too heavily on what I held dear, and I burned with resentment at the treatment given me for what I did. Death! Death for an experiment which could save civilisation, and for which I begged official sanction. Had they given me openly what they let me take by stealth Earth would now hum to the throb of power and the starships would once again soar between the stars."

He turned from the screen and stared down at the limp figure of the old professor. Gently he touched the ruined features and then slowly straightened as the ship sang to the quiver of the nulgrav field. He listened for a moment, his head a little to one side, then made a careful adjustment on the control panel.

"I am no traitor, no embittered individual seeking personal power and fame. What I have I give freely and with both hands. Earth will not own the secret of entropic power, but neither will any one race or star system. Such a secret is too big for any one star. No! Power will be for all, and I shall be the one to give it!"

"I don't understand?" Branson stared at the slender captain, then at the fat engineer. "What do you mean?"

"Ask Jarl. Ask my engineer, he knows, and you are a poor psychologist if you don't know the worth of your own trade. I bear no resentment, and I return bearing gifts. Look!"

He pointed towards the vis-screen and with a startled look at the fat engineer, Branson crowded close to the smooth plastic surface.

A star shone before them, a yellow type-G sun, glowing in the far distance and yet near enough for any space traveller to recognise. The big redheaded man stared at it, imagining that he could see the spinning shapes of familiar worlds, and gripping the edge of the control panel so tightly that the knuckles shone white beneath his freckled skin.

Earth!

The mother world, the home planet, cradle of the race of Man. It lay before them, awaiting the return of her wandering children bearing a new Promethean fire to pour new life into power-starved industries and grounded starships!

Kleon rested his arm across the psychologist's shoulders as together they stared at the distant planet. Softly the ship hummed as it sped across the few remaining miles of the voyage, heading for home.

Home!

Where an old man stared with dying hope at the glittering points of the star-shot sky, and a civilisation waited to welcome its saviour.

www.ingramcontent.com/pod-product-compliance
Lightning Source LLC
Chambersburg PA
CBHW011517170626
46810CB00009B/3398